AN EYE FOR AN EYE

JACK CROSS SI6
BOOK 3

JACK DILLON

ROUGH
EDGES
PRESS

AN EYE FOR AN EYE

AN EYE FOR AN EYE

PROLOGUE

"What do you know of the Hierarchy?" Jack Cross asked as he entered the room.

It was a hotel room not unlike many others in the city, except this particular room held three men whom Jack had traced across England to this location.

The three men in question froze at the sight of the pistol in Jack's hand. It was a Walther PPQ with a suppressor fitted, which meant trouble.

"I don't know what you mean, man," the nearest one blurted out at the sight of the gun aimed at the three of them.

"Let's start with you," Jack said, indicating the calmest-looking one at the back of the room. He was tall with greying hair, but even so, he still looked really fit. Billy Halloran was one of the London gangland's hardest hitters. He had fingers in most things, including gambling, prostitution, and narcotics. The two men with him were Jimmy Halloran, his younger brother, and Nigel Cooke, his minder.

"I don't know who you think you are, coming in here waving that piece around like you own the joint, but let me tell you what's going to happen, shall I?" replied Billy, but the rest of his speech was cut off by the soft cough of the Walther firing. A red mist appeared at the side of his head, and he instantly put his hand up to his ear where the bullet had torn through his flesh.

"I'm sorry, you were saying?" Jack asked calmly.

Cooke made to rush him, but Jack simply shot his knee as he made to move. The bullet slammed into his kneecap, shattering the joint, and he collapsed in agony, both hands clutching at his leg.

"Sit the fuck down," Jack said through gritted teeth. He was beginning to lose his temper with them.

"Now then, Billy, I'm going to tell you what is going to happen. You are going to tell me everything you know about the Hierarchy, or I'll kill all three of you here and now," he said.

Jimmy was panicking now. The two shots had set him off, "But we don't know anything," he screamed.

Jack turned and shot him in the head. The bullet struck him in the center of the forehead, snapping his head back and dropping him to the thick carpet. Cooke, who was behind him, was painted with his blood.

"Then you're no use to me," Jack said.

"You're a dead man, you hear me, a dead man," Billy screamed at him, tears running down his cragged face.

Jack shot him too, in the same way.

That left Cooke the only one left alive.

"Are you going to play nice now and tell me what I want to know, or do I have to shoot you too?" Jack asked, turning his Walther on Cooke.

Pain was etched across the minder's face as he frantically tried to stem the blood flow from his shattered knee. He looked up into the cold stare of the man holding his life in the palm of his hand and swallowed hard.

Jack could tell by the resignation in Cooke's eyes that he wasn't going to learn anything from him. Either he didn't know anything, or he refused to say, the end result would be the same.

"Okay," Jack said, then shot him too.

This seemed to be the way things were going for him lately. He surveyed the scene—just another failed attempt at learning something, *anything*, about the shadowy group responsible for much of his recent troubles, both personal and professional.

Up until now, he had shaken down more than five places and, so far, learned nothing. The only outcome was the trail of bodies he was leaving behind him. Pretty soon, someone was going to notice the trail of chaos he was leaving everywhere and start looking for him, but he couldn't stop, not until he had found something that would lead him to the ones responsible for the deaths of his wife and daughter.

He'd already killed the man who pulled the trigger, but that wasn't enough. He wanted the man who gave the order. He wanted the head of the Hierarchy.

He wouldn't rest, couldn't rest, until he had him in his sights. He had been placed on indefinite leave after the disbanding of SI6, so he had all the time in the world. If need be, he would go to the ends of the earth to find him; he had sworn to kill the man who orchestrated the murder of his family.

He took off the suppressor and returned his pistol to his shoulder rig before leaving the room. He had left no traces behind, he even picked up the empty shell casings from the bullets he'd fired. No one would know he'd been there, and that's how he wanted it to be.

The Hierarchy had caused SI6 to be disbanded so he would return the favor. He would dismantle all their operations and kill as many of their number as he could before the inevitable happened or he rid the world of them. They had taken his life and career from him, leaving him with nothing but time on his hands, so he would devote the rest of his life to destroying them.

Closing the door quietly behind him, he walked down the corridor toward the exit.

CHAPTER ONE

MI6 HQ, LONDON—AUGUST 20

Simon Bennett was a slim man who had a penchant for dark suits. His slicked-back hair was never out of place, and his tie never askew. Appearances were everything in his business, and as the Deputy Director of MI6, he had to be part security wizard and part politician.

Unfortunately, lately, the politics had taken center stage, overshadowing the security aspects of his job. He had overseen the dismantling of SI6 after recent attacks in the center of London by a group now known as the Hierarchy for Anarchy, Terrorism, and Extortion, or HATE, were perpetrated along with an assassination attempt on the Prime Minister himself.

Sir Donald Bainbridge, the head of SI6, had been kidnapped by the Hierarchy and used as bait in an attempt on the PM's life. Bainbridge died from gunshot wounds saving the PM but leaving SI6 leaderless and sacrificed to the public as being responsible for not preventing that and the previous attacks.

Although, at the time, Bennett harbored some resent-ment at the success rate of the rogue group, it was all part of his plan to streamline it and bring it under the control of MI6.

After it was all done and the Hierarchy had paid for the attacks, Bennett informed the survivors of SI6 of his intentions.

He had told them individually what was to happen to them: Commander Dark had an RTU, return to unit, Jack Cross had been given time to grieve being put on indefinite leave, and Robert Deakin was given a position working within MI6. Jennifer Austin had been contacted later and was also absorbed back into MI6. Later and alone, he had told Colonel Armstrong of his plan for him to run a special unit that would only handle missions sanctioned personally by the PM through himself. He hadn't told him any further details at the time simply because he hadn't any. It was still just an idea, one that needed the green light from the PM. So, while the other members of the old SI6 were either on hiatus or working for MI6, he had time to flesh out the idea.

As he sat at his desk, the phone rang at his elbow. As he picked it up, he had no idea how his life was about to change.

"Good morning, Prime Minister. How can I help you?" he said.

Andrew Chambers said, "I prefer to discuss this on a more personal level, Simon. I'll see you in my office in, say, half an hour?"

"I'm on my way, sir," Bennett replied and stood up, grabbing his suit jacket from the back of the chair and shrugging into it as he left the room.

———

His staff car had been waiting for him as he left the building, and he was soon on his way to 10 Downing Street. The police officer on duty allowed him through with just a glance at his ID card. He was then shown through, into the home of the Prime Minister.

As he entered the office, the Prime Minister was seated behind a desk; he looked up and smiled briefly. His dark hair was greying at the temples, and his youthful features were <u>showing</u> signs of wear and tear from the job.

"Take a seat, Simon, and tell me what progress you've made towards setting up your new section," Chambers asked.

Bennett laid it all out, what he had done about procuring a headquarters for the new section and those he was having as staff. After he was done, he waited for the PM's verdict.

"Okay, it all seems fine so far, but I think you need to concentrate on this fully, Simon. I'm replacing you at MI6 to free you up for this new endeavor. You will be the new head of Section Zero. You are to work closely with me and no one else, and your efforts are to be kept off the radar totally. You can work out your own cover story for you and your group, and I will enable funding for you via the security services budget."

Bennett looked at him, waiting for him to finish. "I see, sir," he said finally.

"I have every faith in you, Simon. You are the right man for this job. Bainbridge had a good idea, let's see if you can't improve on it, shall we?"

Bennett nodded his head in agreement as he got to his feet. He knew the meeting was over now. It was time to get the ball rolling and set Section Zero up as a viable outfit.

As he left the office, he looked forward to the challenge he now faced with excitement and a little trepidation too.

————

Colonel Tony Armstrong had been waiting for word from Deputy Director Bennett about when they would start work on the new unit.

It had been more than three weeks since they disbanded SI6, and he was beginning to hear reports of gangland shootings around the city.

These had all the earmarks of professional hits, but when he reached out to his contacts in the Met, there was no hint of any trouble brewing between local gangs. In fact, it had been just the opposite, things had actually quietened down since these killings began. It was as if they were keeping a low profile for fear of bringing attention to themselves.

He began to get suspicious when he hadn't heard anything from Jack. Every time he called him, it went straight to his voicemail, and he had yet to get back to him.

He picked up his phone to check if he'd heard anything back from Jack again when it rang, making him jump.

When he saw who was calling, he felt his pulse begin to race a little faster.

"Good afternoon, Deputy Director Bennett. I've been waiting for your call," he said.

"Come around to my apartment, we have things to discuss," Bennett said.

The call was ended abruptly before Tony could say

anything further, so he put away his phone and grabbed his suit jacket on his way to the door.

Finally, things were going to start happening, and as he closed the door behind him, his stride lengthened with anticipation.

CHAPTER TWO

COLOMBIA—AUGUST 20

Felix Moya looked over the rim of his tumbler. Inside was a deep amber liquid. Taking a sip of the thirty-year-old Macallan Scotch, one of the finest in the world, he asked, "Is everything ready?"

"Yes, Patron, the testing is complete. Doctor Franklin has assured us that this batch is the one," replied Xavier Quesada. He was a brute of a man, standing at an even six feet with broad shoulders and thick arms. His face appeared to have been carved out of granite with a blunt hammer, especially the nose, which was bent out of shape and flattened against his craggy visage. Quesada had been the personal bodyguard to the head of the Moya Cartel for the past twelve years.

"What about the test subject?" Moya asked, putting the tumbler down on the table next to his seat.

"Doctor Franklin assures us he has displayed all the symptoms that he anticipated."

"Good. Inform the manufacturing plant to get the

first shipment fulfilled as quickly as possible. I want it shipped out to be distributed by the end of the week at the latest."

"I'll pass it on, Patron. Will there be anything else?"

"You can tell the chef to serve the Cuadril tonight, cooked the way I like it," Moya said.

He looked across the room where his wife and son sat. His wife, Maria, saw him look and beckoned for her son to follow as she got up and walked over to him. His business was at an end, so she was allowed to be near him.

He watched her walk towards him, her long legs and curvy figure accentuated by the tight dress she wore. She had been a model when they had met twenty years ago and was still as beautiful now as when he first laid eyes on her. Her dark hair was long and flowed down her back, swaying as she approached him. Her deep brown eyes watching him, then glancing at Quesada with fear. At her side was his twelve-year-old son, Marcus. He would grow into a fine man, he was sure. He already had the markings of one. He was good at sports, which he encouraged, and his dark good looks had already made him many fans among the young girls at his private school. He had been allowed home to celebrate his father's upcoming birthday in a few days' time.

Just as they reached him, Quesada put a hand to his ear. Something was coming through his earbud, a communication.

"Patron, there is a vehicle approaching, they stopped short of the gates, now they're just sitting there," he said.

Moya looked up, his interest piqued. "Who is it?" he asked. "Find out what they want."

Before the instruction could be carried out, Moya's

phone rang. He looked at it, recognized the caller ID, and with a wave, halted Quesada from continuing.

"This is a surprise. What do I owe the pleasure of a call from the leader of the Ruiz Cartel?" he asked, looking up into the eyes of his bodyguard. His voice was full of pleasantries, but his eyes told a different story, one of hatred and something else, suspicion. He beckoned his wife and son to sit on the sofa nearby.

"I am reliably informed that you are about to unleash a new product onto the market, one you hope will wipe out the competition," the voice said.

Moya's eyes went wide with fury. Betrayal was permeating through his household, his very family, for that was what he called his close-knit group of confidants, those who knew the intricate details of how he ran his business. Now one of them had betrayed him about his hopes for the new product.

"Who is spreading rumors about me, Roberto?" he replied, sidestepping the question.

"No denials then I see. Okay, seeing as how this is true, here is my message to you..." Roberto Ruiz said, ending the conversation.

Moya was on his feet in a flash. Something was about to go down, and it was going to be messy. If Ruiz was sending a message about being pissed off, it would be direct and to the point. The word 'subtle' just wasn't in his vocabulary.

He snapped a glance at Quesada, who was in contact with the guards at the gate.

Something had happened. He looked back at Moya and said one word that explained it all.

"Incoming!"

Quesada dived at Moya, forcing him to the floor as the wall imploded. Bricks and chunks of pumice were sent spinning into the room as the explosion shattered the side of the huge villa Moya had called home for the past twenty-five years.

The sound of the explosion assailed both their ears. Quesada covered Moya, protecting him with his own body.

"What the hell happened?" Moya wanted to know. His anger overtook his fear of dying.

He looked over the form of Quesada to where his wife and son had been sitting no less than seconds ago. The sofa was covered by large chunks of the wall that had been blown inwards. He could just see an arm protruding out from the rubble, and he knew they were both dead.

Revenge now filled his heart as he pushed the large minder from him.

"The vehicle outside launched a rocket-propelled grenade at the house, Patron," Quesada told him.

"Ruiz will die for this, slowly and with much pain," Moya swore.

As he climbed to his feet, not daring to look at the bodies of his family, he heard gunfire coming from outside the house. He looked around his lounge. It had been almost completely destroyed; one wall was completely gone where the rocket had struck. Debris littered the floor and most of the finer furnishings.

He walked over to the hole in the wall, Quesada at his side with his gun drawn should he need it, ready to step in front of a bullet for his Patron. Outside he could see the front gate and his men firing assault rifles at the vehicle parked beyond.

Bullets peppered it, smashing through the coachwork and windscreen. The doors opened, like wings on a bird of prey, as the driver and front passenger got out, using them for cover. They tried to return fire, but from somewhere out of Moya's line of sight, a rocket flew out, heading right for the SUV.

He could only imagine the shocked expressions on their faces as they watched their doom approach, powerless to do anything to prevent it.

The explosion lifted the vehicle high into the air on a cushion of flames, only to crash down onto the ground once more.

Moya turned away from the hole and began to walk back into the house.

"Make sure the delivery arrives on time," he said.

"What about Ruiz? What do you want me to do about him, Patron?" Quesada asked from behind him.

"Something special."

CHAPTER THREE

Colonel Armstrong rang the bell on the door to Bennett's apartment. He had taken a taxi to this side of the city from his own apartment. As he stood on the doorstep looking up at the white-fronted Georgian townhouse that Bennett lived in, it brought home to him just how big the difference was in their pay scale.

The intercom buzzed, allowing him access to the interior of the building. He opened the large front door and entered the hallway.

Bennett appeared at the end of the hallway framed in the doorway to the lounge, backlit by the lamps inside, giving him somewhat of an ethereal quality.

"There you are, Colonel," he said, beckoning him forward.

Tony walked down the hallway and entered the lounge. Before him was a large Adam fireplace restored to its initial glory with an array of photos, mostly of the family, arranged on the mantelpiece. The white leather three-piece was modern and looked comfortable. Bennett stood by a sideboard that had a tray of tumblers on top with a few bottles of spirits to accompany them.

"Can I get you a drink before we begin?" he asked.

"Scotch, please," Tony replied, feeling slightly uncomfortable by this blatant show of wealth. He was aware that Bennett had connections, but he had no idea just how far they went or how deep.

Bennett passed over a tumbler of a rich amber liquid. "Here, try this," he said.

Tony held it to his nose. The first thing he noticed was how sweet it was, then the vanilla notes reached his nostrils. Taking a sip, he was surprised at the exotic fruits that came through with an earthy richness before the creamy finish. He smiled, it really was rather nice.

"This is a new one to my collection. It's a Bruichladdich Black Art aged for twenty-four years. What do you think?"

"It's fine, thanks, but I doubt you brought me here for a tasting," Tony replied, wanting to get to the point of this meeting, his unease showing through.

"Down to business it is then," Bennett said. "I've just had a lengthy conversation with Prime Minister Chambers. We talked in detail about the future, in particular mine and that of this new unit, or rather, section. I am to head up Section Zero, a small department tasked with extreme missions sanctioned only by the PM himself."

"Section Zero, so is this going to be the new SI6?" Tony asked.

"In a way, but in another, not. Section Zero will have the full backing of the PM, which comes with complete funding but only as long as we produce results," explained Bennett.

"So, are we part of MI6 now then?" Tony asked, a

little concerned about the restraints this would come with should they be part of the larger organization.

"No, we will be part of the Security Services but a whole different section. Our profile will be non-existent; it will appear as if we are working off the books, as it were. We have to distance ourselves from the rest of the security services, so our headquarters will be separate also," Bennett explained before he took another sip of his drink.

"Where will we be based then?"

"There is a new development in Canary Wharf, an office block. The ground floor and basement will be assigned to us. I'll give you the address before you leave. It will have everything you and your group will need. The basement will be fully soundproofed and stocked with whatever your Armourer requires, and the communications will be connected to every network available, as will your tech section. Deakin will have whatever he needs to do his job."

"Last question, when do we start?" Tony asked.

Bennett gave him a puzzled look. "I thought you'd ask who would be in this section first."

"I just assumed we'd use the old crew from SI6, Jen on comms, and you already mentioned Robert for IT and the Major as Armourer along with Jack Cross once he returns to duty. Are you saying that we'll be using someone else?"

"No, you assumed correctly, and to that effect, I suggest you find out where Jack is and what he's been up to," Bennett replied.

"Copy that, sir. I'll get right on it. So, sir, when do we start?" Tony asked again.

"You start right now, Colonel. Welcome to Section Zero."

CHAPTER FOUR

CHARLOTTE, NORTH CAROLINA, US—AUGUST 21

Jack entered the bar and spotted Mike Flynn right away, seated at the front, talking to the barman.

Sitting down on the free bar stool next to him, he asked, "How you doing, Mike?"

Mike turned around, a smile stretching across his rugged features. "Jack, my God, it's good to see you, buddy. I'm doin' fine, my man. More to the point, how are you doin'? Is it true they disbanded SI6?" he asked.

Jack waved the barman over, ordered a Scotch on the rocks, then turned to his friend. "After the attacks and Bainbridge's death, someone had to pay, so they shut us down, or rather Deputy Director of MI6 Bennett shut us down. I'm on extended leave until they figure out what to do with me," he said.

"And what have you been doin'? My gut tells me you've not been takin' it easy?" Mike asked.

"This and that, you know me, Mike. I like to keep busy."

"What are you not tellin' me, Jack?"

He thought about what to tell him. They had been partners for years and had shared almost everything about their lives, so it felt strange keeping things from him.

"I've been chasing down any lead I can to the Hierarchy. I want to know who was behind the hit on me and my family, but so far, I've drawn a complete blank," he said, deciding to tell him everything. If he couldn't trust him, then who could he trust?

"So, what's your next move, buddy?" Mike asked.

"That's just it, Mike, I have no idea."

"Hi guys, can I join you?" a voice said from over Jack's shoulder. He turned to see who it was, and a lovely face smiled back at him.

Mike said, "What the hell are you doin' here, Charley?"

Jack turned fully in his seat to get a better look at the woman who had made Mike smile so wide. She was in her early thirties, he assumed, but he couldn't be sure as her skin was flawless. Her short, flaming-red hair reached no further than her shoulders and framed a face that was open and friendly. Eyes the color of polished mahogany sparkled when she smiled, and she seemed to do that a lot when she looked at Mike. She was wearing a short leather bomber jacket over a white blouse, under which he could tell was hidden a well-toned body. Her jeans were tight and fitted around all her curves; this was a woman who took pride in her body and kept in shape.

"Charlotte Parker, I'd like you to meet Jack Cross, my old buddy from England," Mike said, introducing him.

"Less of the 'old', Mike. You'll put her off wanting to talk to me," Jack chastised. He offered a hand to her, saying, "Pleased to meet you."

"Only my mother and Mike, when he wants to piss me off, call me Charlotte. My friends call me Charley," she replied, smiling broadly as she took the offered hand.

"You never answered my question, Charley. What are you doin' around these parts?" Mike asked again.

"Same as you, Mike, taking a break from work," she replied, but Jack could tell she was hiding something.

"Oh, you can talk freely around Jack, he's one of us. We worked together for years, so he's cool," Mike told her quietly.

"I know you used to be in Delta, Mike, so how come you worked with a Brit? Was it some kinda special unit type thing you had goin' on?"

"Kinda," Mike confirmed.

"What are you, CIA?" Jack asked her changing the subject slightly away from who they both had worked for. He didn't think it appropriate, especially as how SI6 had been disbanded.

"DEA," she replied finally.

"So, what're you doin' all the way over here? I thought you worked the Miami beat." Mike asked.

"Took some time off to visit family while I wait for something to develop in the case I'm working."

"How are your family?" Mike asked.

"They're good. I have a place of my own near them so I can check in on them from time to time; they're not getting any younger, you know."

"Aren't we all... So what's this case you're working?"

"Can't we just hang? I'm off duty for a couple of hours before I have to get back to work," she said, avoiding the question.

Jack looked at her and then at Mike, who was about to argue, about to push for an answer, so he intervened.

"Of course we can. Let me get you a drink," he said, waving the bartender over.

"Tell you what, let's go grab a bite. I'm buying," she countered, waving the bartender off.

Mike said, "You had me at 'I'm buying'."

CHAPTER FIVE

COLOMBIA

Felix Moya stood at the door to the morgue, apprehensive about what he was about to do.

He'd seen death many times, had caused more than his fair share, but this was different. This time he was here to identify the bodies of his wife and son before they were sent to the funeral director for preparation for the funeral.

It was something he knew he had to do, but still, he wished with all his heart it had never happened.

As always, Quesada was at his side. More now than ever before, he felt he needed the big man's support. Since the attack, his minder had not let him out of his sight, even to the point of following him to the bathroom.

"Are you ready, Patron?" Quesada asked gently at his side.

Moya gave a nod and slowly entered the room. It was cold, almost like an icebox, and the medical examiner was standing by the tables that had the bodies laid out with white sheets draped over them. He had managed to prevent the autopsies from being performed, he already knew the cause of death, and his influence with the police had overruled the law this time.

As he approached, the ME uncovered each body and then stepped back towards the doorway to allow him the privacy he required.

Standing between the two tables, he looked at each of them in turn and was surprised at how calm they appeared. No trace of the violent act that terminated their young lives was evident on their faces. They could be asleep, but he knew they weren't. He knew they would never awake from this slumber, that he had been robbed of any future they might have spent together. It was lost to him now, but he vowed to have his revenge on the one responsible for this act.

Holding back the tears took an enormous effort. His body shook with that effort, and finally, he brought himself under control. Angry with himself for allowing one single tear to escape and run slowly down his cheek, he quickly wiped it away, dismissing it as a lapse.

From now on, he would focus all his attention on revenge.

Ruiz would pay for this and pay dearly. He had taken his wife and son from him, so now he would return the favor. He would take everything Ruiz loved from him and destroy them one by one until he had nothing left, and then, when he was left with nothing but memories, he would end him too.

This he swore on the lives of his dead family.

Turning from the bodies, he walked to the door.

"Have them made ready for the funeral. I want an

open casket ceremony, so ensure they look their best for their final viewing," he said to the ME at the door.

"It will be done, Patron," the ME replied, bowing in reverence to him.

Moya walked to the entrance and out into the sunlight. It was a new day filled with opportunities, but he only had dark thoughts, and until his thirst for revenge had been sated, he knew this would not change.

CHAPTER SIX

CHARLOTTE, NORTH CAROLINA, US

The three of them were seated in the restaurant, one of the local eateries in the area that served good local cuisine.

They had chosen a table over by the wall, away from the center of the large room, so they could talk freely without fear of being overheard. This was their time off, so they wanted to enjoy it undisturbed.

Drinks were delivered to the table while they decided what to order from the food menu.

Jack looked down the list and chose a steak, medium rare with all the trimmings. Mike chose the same, while Charley had the ribs.

"So, Mike, how are you feeling? I heard they took you off the active roster?" Charley asked, looking at him pointedly.

Jack noticed the way she looked at him, there was history there, but he wasn't sure what it was.

"How did you know about that?" he asked.

"I have my sources, you know that. All I know is that you were involved in some kinda accident, and you were injured. You don't have to go into too much detail. I know the work you did was classified, so have they?" she said.

"Yes, damn it. They said there were complications in my recovery. Apparently, my spleen was damaged in the accident, they thought they repaired it, but soon after, I had a minor relapse and they had to remove part of it. Now that I'm compromised health-wise, they decided to give me a chair to shine with my ass," Mike explained.

"You're okay though, right?" Jack asked.

"I'm fine, buddy, I'll never be able to go on the front line again, but I can still enjoy a normal life, as long as I take it easy, their words, not mine."

The food arrived, cutting that particular topic of conversation dead, much to Mike's obvious relief.

"So, how long have you two known each other?" Jack asked as he slipped a piece of his steak into his mouth.

"Through a third party," Charley said too enigmatically for Jack's taste.

"What's that supposed to mean?"

Mike answered for her, "I dated Charley's sister for a time."

Jack nodded his understanding. It all fit, the sideways glances, the odd looks.

"And you never really appreciated just what a catch Mike really was or how lucky your sister was?" Jack said, smiling.

He caught the glance she gave him, then she broke down and smiled.

"Something like that."

"So, what's it like over at the DEA?" Jack asked, throwing her off her stride a little.

"Oh, you know, chasing bad guys and all that," she said, hoping he would leave it at that.

"Ever heard of the Hierarchy?" he asked.

The pause told him she had.

"The Hierarchy for Anarchy, Terrorism, and Extortion or HATE. Your face tells me you have," he pushed.

"Okay, yes, we've heard of them, but mostly just whispers and rumors. They have long arms which reach quite a long way," she said finally.

"You can say that again," Jack agreed.

"I take it you've had a run-in with them?" she observed.

"More than once," Jack agreed.

"They're the reason I'm no longer on active duty," Mike added.

"So, what do you want from me? I don't know much, like I said, just rumors, really." Charley said.

"I would appreciate anything you have. The people I used to work for have a vested interest in them. If I can give them anything on them, it might put me back in their good books."

"Have you been a bad boy, Jack?" she asked with a smile.

"Something like that," he confirmed with a shy smile.

Charley gave a long sigh. "I'll do what I can, but no promises. Like I said, I don't know much."

Jack glanced across the table at Mike, who was giving him the 'leave it' look.

"Thanks, whatever you have, I'm sure it will be helpful," Jack said, smiling to diffuse the tension that was building.

"Can we continue with our meal now?" she asked, returning his smile.

The rest of the meal continued with good-natured

banter of passing stories around the table of past exploits without too much detail and smiles all around.

When it was time to leave, Charley agreed to pay the bill as promised.

"Come on, guys, it's my treat. I have an expense account anyway, so no big deal."

"Next time, I'll pay then," Jack said, which Charley pounced on. "Okay then, I will hold you to that. I don't know when, but the next time, this is on you."

"Careful buddy looks like she has her hooks into you already," Mike joked.

Dismissing the comment with a wave, Charley asked, "Where you headed now?"

"To the airport to catch a flight back home," Jack told her.

"Me too, let's share a cab," she said.

"I have to go grab my bag at the hotel first," Jack said as if to put her off.

"Cool, perhaps we could grab a drink in the bar before going on to the airport?"

"I'll leave you two to sort out the logistics of your next step. I'm off, back to my apartment. Take care, buddy, and don't do anything I wouldn't, ok?"

———

Outside the restaurant, Jack hailed a cab, and they both climbed in the back. He gave the driver the address of his hotel, and they sat back and relaxed.

Charley's phone rang, and she tensed as she saw who was calling.

Jack reached forward and slid the partition between the driver and passenger sections closed so they could talk in private.

"Parker here, go ahead," she said.

Jack could tell by the way her whole demeanor had changed that this was work-related.

"I see, sir. I can be back at base in a few hours. I'll catch the first flight out," she said, not giving much away.

There was a pause again as she listened.

"Charlotte," she said.

Another pause.

"I'll be there, sir," she said, then hung up.

Jack was looking away during the call, but as she put away her phone, he turned to face her.

"I have to go back to work, they're sending a chopper to pick me up," she said.

"Must be serious then," Jack observed.

"It is. Things are about to erupt in Colombia. We suspect a new drug war is on the horizon, and I've been called back in."

"Do we have time for me to pick up my stuff?" he asked.

"Absolutely, the chopper won't get here for some time yet, I think, but then I'll have to leave you. I'm sorry. Maybe we can grab that drink another time, say in a few weeks maybe?"

"I don't see why not. I'll look forward to it," he said, surprising himself because he actually meant it.

"Cool," she said, smiling.

Before long, they had arrived at his hotel, where he jumped out of the taxi, ran into the hotel to grab his bag, then returned, slamming the door closed as he got in.

"There's an extra fifty in it for you if you get us to the airport in the next half hour," he told the driver.

Spurred on by the extra tip, he peeled away from the curb into traffic and sped down the road.

They arrived at the airport well within the allotted

half hour, and Jack paid the driver his fee plus the extra fifty dollars they'd agreed on.

Charley was waiting on the curb, looking around to ensure no one was listening.

"Look, Jack, I feel I ought to warn you. I can't go into any details, but if you have any contacts in the Drug Squad back home, then you should warn them that something big is coming," she said, looking intensely into his blue eyes.

"Something big as in a war or perhaps something new on the market? Can you give me something more, anything?" Jack asked.

"It could be both, and that's all I'm gonna say. I've probably said too much as it is. If my boss in the DEA finds out I said anything at this stage, he'll have my ass," she said as her eyebrows pinched together in concern.

Jack smiled briefly, which she caught. "What?" she asked.

"Oh, nothing," Jack said, dismissing it.

"No, go on. What did you find so funny about my boss chewing my ass off?"

Again, Jack smiled then, with a straight face, said, "Well, it is a nice ass."

She playfully punched his arm, "You're such a wise ass," she said, trying to hide her smile with indignation.

The sound of a chopper coming in to land broke through their conversation. It swooped in and landed outside the terminal, the letters 'DEA' emblazoned across the side of the aircraft.

"Subtle," he said.

She turned to him and hurriedly said, "What's your number?"

He dutifully told her. She quickly opened her own

phone and tapped furiously away on the keypad before looking back at him.

"I will text you, then you will have my number, so there's no excuse for you not to call me," she said before she turned and ran to the waiting chopper.

Jack watched her get aboard and wave before the rotors spooled up, gaining enough momentum to lift off.

He could still see her smiling face in the window as the craft lifted high into the air before it banked over and then sped off into the darkening skies.

His phone had vibrated in his hand as she ran across the tarmac to the chopper. He looked again as it vibrated once more, and a text appeared on the screen, it read, 'Don't forget, next time, the drinks are on you.'

He hefted his bag in his hand as he read the text, then turned to enter the terminal. For the first time in a while, he found he enjoyed the company of another woman. What surprised him the most was that he didn't feel at all guilty about it. He knew Melissa would not want him spending the rest of his days mourning her. Life was for living, and all that either of them had ever wanted for the other, was for them to be happy.

As he walked through the terminal, he realized that for the first time in months, that's exactly what he was, happy.

CHAPTER SEVEN

COLOMBIA

Doctor Rupert Franklin was worried. In fact, he was downright terrified.

He had done everything Moya wanted, but he had his own agenda, and now he had to get out before the man learned the truth. If that happened, or *when*, he was a dead man for sure.

He knew he had a chance of escaping, and this recent attack by Ruiz had caused Moya to switch his concentration onto his old adversary with one goal, revenge.

Moya was marshaling his forces to go on the attack, and this was Franklin's chance to escape. He would depart during all the confusion of the men leaving to attack Ruiz's compound.

He went nowhere without the man Moya had appointed as his guardian while he did his work formulating the new drug recipe. This man was Luis Sancho, but he was also his confidante. He was working with the DEA, much the same as he was, and Sancho was sympathetic to what Franklin was doing. He made sure he was the man appointed to watch over him. They soon cultivated a working relationship, and when Franklin told him he wanted out, he made the necessary arrangements. This attack from Ruiz had been down to his leaking the news of Moya's plans to him, hoping for the exact same result and Moya's reaction. He had played a dangerous game, but it seemed to be working.

There was a convoy of four vehicles lined up in the driveway, waiting to leave. He walked over to the back of the convoy, where another SUV was parked, and got in. Sancho was in the driver's seat.

"Are you ready for this?" Sancho asked.

Franklin simply nodded, his fear making it difficult for him to even speak.

"Let's go then," Sancho said and started the SUV.

As the convoy drove towards the exit, they joined behind, falling in line with them.

As they neared the gate, his palms were slick with sweat, and he wiped them on the legs of his pants. Praying the guards wouldn't question them and regard them as part of the convoy, they kept pace with the other vehicles.

The gate loomed closer, and the guards stood back as the vehicles drove past, the lights from the guard hut illuminating them. Franklin held his breath as they reached the gates where the guards stood watch, but nothing happened. As he kept his gaze fixed firmly ahead, he saw in his peripheral vision that they didn't even glance his way. They left the villa grounds behind as the convoy drove on, and he let out the breath he had been holding in for so long.

Still not out of the woods yet, they dropped back slightly, allowing the SUV in front of them to get farther away. Watching his side mirror, Franklin kept a watch on the villa. When he couldn't see it anymore as the night closed in, Sancho took the first turning off, leaving the convoy to continue without them.

Time was not on his side. As soon as Moya learned of his departure, he would send men to bring him back. Sancho drove towards a private airfield run by one of Moya's men, who Sancho had assured him had agreed to take him wherever he wanted. He had planned this for some time, and so far, everything was going according to plan, in fact, better than he had planned. Being able to leave had always been a stumbling block in his plan, and he had been wracking his brain on how he would pull it off. Leaving the planning to Sancho had been a godsend for him.

Forty minutes after leaving the villa, they were pulling up at the private airfield. Leaving the SUV in the parking area, Franklin and Sancho crossed the tarmac towards the small private plane. It was an old Cessna Skyhawk single-engine craft that was predominantly used as a training plane.

The pilot was standing, waiting for them by the Cessna.

"Is everything ready for take-off?" Sancho asked as they stopped at the side of the plane.

The pilot, Alvarez Kelly, nodded before saying, "Of course. Are you sure this has been sanctioned by Patron?"

"You can call him and ask him if you like. I'm sure he'll take the time out from his busy schedule of planning the revenge of his dead wife and son to talk to you over this routine visit," Sancho said calmly.

Kelly looked at him, then at Franklin, who looked away for fear his own nerves would give the game away.

This was a bluff that Sancho had assured him would work should Kelly ask about the validity of their trip.

After a pause, Kelly said, "I'll not bother him with details like this. Climb aboard and we'll take off then."

Franklin did as he was told, and when he was seated in the seat behind the pilot next to Sancho, he strapped himself into the chair. The engine spooled up, and the large propeller in front spun faster as it gained momentum. Gradually they started to move, taxiing down the runway and picking up speed as they traveled. Pretty soon, they had enough momentum for lift-off. Kelly pulled back on the control stick, and the nose of the plane lifted off the ground.

Franklin clutched the armrests of his seat as the nose lifted, followed by the rest of the aircraft. In a few seconds, they were airborne, and Franklin was moving farther away from the villa, leaving his past far behind him.

———

COLOMBIA

Felix Moya had driven through the night with his convoy to Ruiz's compound. They had chosen to arrive as the sun came up to catch Ruiz and his men off guard.

Moya had at his disposal two attack helicopters, which were on call, ready for this assault. They were stationed nearby, ready to move on his word.

He took out his phone. The call he was about to make would put into motion events that would be impossible to reverse. Vengeance cried out to him, the deaths of his wife and son cried out to be answered, and in Colombia, there could only be one answer.

His finger trembled over the call button, not with trepidation but with anticipation. He was eager to see his enemies crushed beneath his bootheels.

He pressed the button, and the call was connected.

"Go!" One word was all he said. One word was all that was needed to set things moving, and the attack choppers would move in to rain hellfire and damnation down on Ruiz and his followers.

A phone went off to his side and was answered. He only half heard the conversation as all his focus was on waiting for the choppers to fly overhead and begin.

"Patron, Doctor Franklin has left the villa with Sancho," a voice said in his ear.

Not quite understanding what had been said, he turned to look at the man who had taken the call.

"What?" he asked.

The man swallowed hard before speaking, clearly afraid of delivering the bad news, "Doctor Franklin and Sancho have both left the villa, Patron. No one knows where they have gone."

Franklin was vital to his operation, and for him to leave so suddenly was disastrous.

"Find them," he said, turning to look through the SUV's side window as the sound of choppers alerted him to what would happen next.

He turned back to the man who had taken the call, now he could devote the proper attention to this problem.

"Ping his phone, then send out a team to follow him. I want them both found and brought back to the villa, alive," he said. "I will deal with them personally."

CHAPTER EIGHT

"You know, Wendy, this could work," Jack said after viewing the entire apartment.

He'd arrived back at Heathrow Airport later the previous night and had gone straight to his hotel room. He'd moved out of the family home shortly after the funerals, as being there was just too painful for him. Deciding on the morning of the funerals to put the house on the market, he had contacted an estate agent at his earliest convenience.

Spending the night in his room, he left the next morning, immediately after having breakfast in the hotel dining room, to go and view an apartment the estate agent had sourced for him. Wendy Taylor, the estate agent, had left a message on his voicemail about the viewing, which he read as he got off the plane the night before, and he called her while he had been waiting for a taxi to take him to the hotel.

The apartment was in a three-story Victorian terrace

that had been converted into several apartments or flats. He met her upstairs in the apartment, where she showed him the lounge/diner. She started her presentation by saying, "Look, Jack, I know there's no point in pressuring you, so I'll wait here and just let you take a look around. Take your time, there's no rush."

He looked around at the two bedrooms, the master had an en-suite with a king-size bed and large built-in wardrobes. The separate bathroom had all the facilities, including a shower over the bath. The kitchen was fitted with every convenience needed to run an orderly kitchen, including a dishwasher, washer, tumble dryer, cooker, and fridge freezer.

The lounge had a smart three-piece white leather suite that was both stylish and comfortable.

"Do you want me to draw up the papers?" Wendy asked, suppressing a slight smile.

Before Jack could reply, his phone rang. He recognized the ID and turned to Wendy, "Please do. I'm sorry I have to take this."

He left the room, heading for the master bedroom and closing the door behind him so he wouldn't be overheard, even though his mobile was coded and protected against eavesdropping. "Tony, what can I do for you?"

"How have you been, Jack?" Tony asked.

"Nice of you to ask, Colonel. Actually, I'm better than I have been for a while and ready to go back to work."

"I'm glad to hear that, Jack, because we are setting up a new section which I want you to be part of. I'll send you a text with the address of our new HQ. You can meet me there as soon as you've finished viewing your new apartment," Tony said, surprising Jack.

How the fuck did he know that?

"Am I under surveillance, sir?" he asked.

"What do you think, Captain? You may be on extended leave, but I had to ensure that you were okay."

"Right, sir. I should be done in a few moments, and then I'll be there."

As he left the bedroom, he saw Wendy still in the lounge working on her phone. A thought immediately struck him, was it Wendy who was watching him? Dismissing the thought, he said, "I have to go back to work. Can you have the papers ready today, please? I'd like to move in as soon as possible."

"I'll draw them up as soon as I return to the office. I can have them ready by the end of the day. You should be able to move in in a few days if that's okay," she said.

"That's fine, thanks," he said, then looked at his phone again as a text came in showing an address. He knew where this was and, as he looked up, he said, "I'm really sorry, but I have to go. Like I said, it's work. Thanks for your time, Wendy. As soon as you have the papers ready, let me know, and I'll pop around to sign them." With a wave, he bid her goodbye and left the apartment.

CHAPTER NINE

MIAMI—AUGUST 22

Charley looked out at the expanse of water before her. The Florida Keys were out there somewhere beyond her line of sight, and that was the direction they would be coming from. The small plane carrying Franklin and his contact, Luis Sancho, would be arriving soon, and she had to be ready to move the moment they landed.

She had arrived in Miami the night before and had been booked into a hotel for the night. Her handler, Bill Harper, told her they would have an early start and to get some rest which she eagerly complied with.

This operation had been a closely guarded secret within the DEA because the drug cartels were notorious not only for having moles implanted within all federal agencies but for their ruthlessness in dealing with anyone who crossed them. It was not unheard of for an agent's family to also be targeted when they learned of his betrayal. They dealt a swift and memorable death to all those involved and sometimes to those who weren't. It was all about sending out a message to everyone that you did not mess with cartel business. It was a message that was well received and understood. Getting anyone to turn on them was nigh on impossible, and that was why the DEA had gone to extraordinary lengths to cultivate Franklin. His testimony would put away Moya for life, the implications of which would possibly close down his cartel for decades.

She saw it then, coming in low over the horizon as the sun glinted off the water.

Dressed for business, she had on a pair of jeans with a white tee shirt, over which she had on a thin jacket, just enough to cover her shoulder rig in which she carried her service weapon, a Glock 23, along with three extra clips.

The sun was high enough for the heat to spread across the water, and she slipped on a pair of Ray-Bans to cut out the glare from the sun hitting the water.

Knowing where the plane would land, she got back in her rental vehicle, a Ford SUV, and started the engine. If today went well, this could be a career-defining moment for her, and she would shoot up the ladder in the department.

That was later though, let's just get through the day first.

Pulling up the Ford at the side of the private landing strip frequently used by Moya and his men, she watched as the small Cessna taxied to a stop and the door opened.

The first person out of the plane was Sancho, who she recognized straight away from his photos on record. They had never met in person but had communicated frequently by phone and email. The second person through the door was Franklin, and even from this distance, she could see the frightened, wide-eyed glare like that of a rabbit caught in the headlights of an oncoming vehicle.

As she started walking down towards the plane, she heard the approaching sound of another vehicle, this one was coming at a speed. Immediately her hackles rose.

Something was very wrong with this picture.

No one was supposed to know about this meet, so how come these guys were here?

Turning around, she headed back to the SUV and climbed back inside. The engine growled to life, and she gunned the engine as she steered it towards the parked Cessna. The fast approach of the SUV spooked both Sancho and Franklin, and she saw them both start to look around, confusion written all over their faces.

In her rearview, she could see the other vehicle pick up even more speed. A figure appeared leaning out of the side window, holding something she couldn't quite make out from this distance, but it was pointed in her direction.

Bullets zinged past her side window as she realized what the guy was holding. Her side mirror shattered as a bullet tore right through it.

Slamming her foot down hard on the gas pedal, she aimed the SUV at the Cessna.

Spinning the large vehicle around into a side spin, she stopped the SUV sideways onto the Cessna.

"Get in!" she shouted through her open side window.

Sancho pushed Franklin towards the SUV and climbed in after him.

"What's going on? Who are those guys?" Sancho asked as she sped away from the plane.

More bullets hit the plane's fusillade and the ground where the SUV had been just moments before.

"How the hell did these guys learn about this meet? I thought this was kept on the down low." Sancho asked.

"I was gonna ask you the same thing," Charley

replied, keeping an eye on her rearview as the other vehicle, another SUV, turned to come after them.

"There has to be a leak somewhere," Sancho insisted.

Franklin asked, "What happens now?"

"Now, we keep on running until we get away," Charley told him. "Are you carrying?" she asked Sancho.

He pulled out a Glock to show her.

"I suggest you point it out the window at those motherfuckers who're shooting at us then," she advised. "We can discuss how they found us later when we get clear of them."

Franklin was terrified, she could see by his wide-eyed stare as it flashed around the interior of the SUV and back out through the window at the vehicle chasing them.

She felt the wind from the window blow into the cab as Sancho opened it. He leaned out and fired back towards the chasing SUV with his Glock. The bullets being fired sounded like loud pops from inside the cab as the speed they were traveling ripped the effect from them.

The road ahead was coming to an end, and she had to leave the private airfield and return to the road which would lead them to the interior of Miami. This was something she really didn't want to happen, and those following knew that. Charley saw them swerve out of the range of gunfire being poured at them from the passenger side of the SUV and increase their speed.

"They're gaining ground on us, Sancho. You'd better do something and fast," she screamed as loud as she could.

Holding the wheel one-handed, she reached for her own Glock. Placing it on her knees, she opened the window with her free hand while steering the SUV with her other. Picking up her Glock once more, she glanced through her rearview to see where the trailing vehicle was, then put her free arm through the window and, aiming blindly, fired at the SUV behind.

Remarkably, because the trailing vehicle had swerved towards her side of the SUV to get away from Sancho's gunfire, they had run straight into Charley's range. She was amazed to see her bullets all strike the windshield of the vehicle behind them. The glass starred from the impacts, and suddenly, the vehicle turned savagely across the shortening road.

Before the steering could be corrected, the SUV flipped, rolling sideways down the road behind them, bouncing and rolling, smashing the roof down on those inside.

She pulled her arm inside as a smile spread across her face, she couldn't believe her luck. At least one of her shots must have hit the driver, and he had lost control of the SUV, and they had crashed.

As they were no longer being pursued, they were free to continue to the end of the road inside the airfield and join the outer roads.

"What the fuck just happened?" Sancho asked as he sat facing forward, his eyes wide in shock.

"We got lucky is what happened," Charley replied. She felt the adrenaline still coursing through her body as she drove off the airfield towards Miami. She kept a watch on her rearview, but there was no sign of them being followed now that the vehicle had crashed.

Whoever sent them obviously thought one vehicle would be enough to handle them. Their purpose had been unclear; they had only opened fire when they saw them escaping. Had their shots been to force them to stop or something more ruthless? They would never know until she found out what their objective had been, and she wasn't going to go back and ask, not now. Her main objective was to get Franklin somewhere safe, but she also had Sancho to consider. His cover had been blown, or had it? There was no way of knowing who had sent those guys after them. She had assumed it had been Moya, but what if it hadn't been him? If it hadn't been him, then who else could it have been?

These were questions she would have the answers to only when she learned more about what was going on. Right now, she would have to inform her handler about the new situation.

She took out her phone and called Harper.

"Bill, this turned out to be a clusterfuck," she said quickly.

"What the hell do you mean?" he asked after a short pause which did not go unnoticed.

"Someone came to meet the plane, and they weren't too happy about us leaving," she explained cryptically.

Another pause before Harper spoke again. "Where are you now?"

She told him their whereabouts, and he said, "Okay, go to the address I'm going to give you, it's a safe house, and wait for further instructions."

"What are you going to do, Bill? Send us some backup? We need another exfil because we can't take the chance that the existing one hasn't been compromised," she replied.

"Don't worry, Charley, everything will work out. I've got this. Just get to the safe house. I'll do everything else," Harper said and ended the call.

She knew he liked to keep his cards close to his chest, but there was something about his response that had her worried.

Was it leftover residue from the recent attack or something more?

Her training was telling her to trust the chain of command, but her gut was telling her something else completely.

She dialed another number on her phone, one she had recently stored in her memory. When it was answered, she said, "Jack, I need your help."

CHAPTER TEN

LONDON

Jack looked at his phone. This was not the call he was expecting from her, but it was one he would respond to either way. When he met her, he had an idea that their experiences together would be different and exciting, but this was not quite what he had in mind.

He put his phone away and looked at Tony; they were at the new HQ on Canary Wharf. They had met there as per his previous conversation with the Chief of Staff.

"What do you think?" Tony asked, clearly interested.

"Well, sir, she works for the DEA and is a trusted friend of Mike's. Apart from that, I'm not sure I can help much more. We met, had a very pleasant time together, agreed to meet again in a few weeks when we both had some free time. Basically, that's it. She steered the conversation away from work at every opportunity, which you'd expect from a good operative. One thing she did mention though... Before we arrived at the airport, she received a call, she said it was work-related. Now, I only heard her side of the conversation, and she was guarded in what she said, but as we said goodbye, she said something that got me thinking. She said that if I had contacts in the Drug Squad back home to inform them that something was coming, something big. When I questioned her about if it was a war or something new, she said it could be both."

Tony asked the million-dollar question, "So what do you plan on doing about this phone call?"

"With your permission, sir, I'd like Robert to look into her activities to see if we can find out a bit more about what she's been working on. The fact that she contacted me makes me think she could be suspicious of those in her department. While Robert looks into all that, I'll catch the next flight to Miami and see if I can find out more when I get on the ground."

"You'll do no such thing," Tony said emphatically. Jack squared his shoulders, ready to argue. "Excuse me, sir—" he started, but Tony waved off any further comments.

"You'll take the Gulfstream. It'll be far quicker than going through normal channels. She's fuelled and waiting at Fairfax as we speak," he said.

"Thank you, sir," Jack said with a surprised smile.

"Take my car, just tell the driver to come back and pick me up when he's done," Tony said finally.

"Yes, sir, I'll call her as soon as I'm on board to see if I can find out more of what's going on, then give you a sit-rep."

"Okay, get going. We can do the viewing of this new HQ properly on your return," Tony said. Jack nodded his agreement and walked towards the door.

———

MIAMI

Charley drove to the address Bill had texted her and pulled up in the car park opposite. It was a small apartment block close to the beach that she knew the DEA had used before.

"Come on, let's get inside and see what happens," she instructed the others.

"I don't like this...if Moya finds me, I'm a dead man, you know that. So why aren't we as far away from here as possible?" Franklin whined as he got out of the SUV, frantically looking around him.

"Try and appear as natural as possible, shall we? If anyone is watching us, then you looking around like that, acting all furtive and suspicious, will certainly give them something to think about, don't you think?" she told him calmly and quietly.

Sancho agreed with Franklin, "He's right, you know, this is a bad idea. Staying this close to Miami just gives them a better chance of finding us."

"Look, I'm just following orders, now get inside while I make a call," she said sternly.

Sancho threw his hands up and turned back to the SUV. "Give me the keys. If you want to remain here, go ahead. I'm getting the hell away from here. Moya knows me, knows what I look like, and if I stay here, I'm a dead man for sure."

"You're going nowhere. You're going to get inside like the rest of us and see this through to the end," she argued.

"Screw you, Charley, you can stay if you like, but not me. I'm off," he said, standing his ground.

She tossed him the keys to the SUV.

"Go ahead then, do what you have to, but I thought you had bigger balls than this, Sancho."

"Clearly not as big as yours, Charley. See you around," he said as he caught the keys in mid-air and ran back to the SUV.

Charley watched as he gunned the engine and took off down the street in a squeal of burning rubber.

"Come on, let's get inside," she told Franklin. If Moya was after them, then they would know what vehicle they were traveling in so Sancho wouldn't get too far without them locating him. He may just have given them some extra breathing space without realizing it.

As they entered the small residence after inputting the command code to unlock the door and disarm the alarm, she called Bill Harper once more.

"Okay, Bill, we're here, so now what?" she said when he came on the line.

"Now you stay where you are until the other team gets there to bring you out," he said.

"Any news on how they found out Franklin would be landing at that particular strip?" she asked, moving out of earshot of her charge.

"Don't worry about that now," Bill evaded.

"What are you not telling me, Bill?" she persisted.

"Nothing. Look, we're working on it from this end. You concentrate on keeping you and Franklin safe, okay?"

"Copy that," she said and hung up the call.

Something was wrong here, but she couldn't put her finger on what it was. She had her doubts, but without any proof, there was no way she could verify what her gut was telling her. The thing was, the only way to prove what she was thinking was for her and Franklin to die.

CHAPTER ELEVEN

WASHINGTON DC

Bill Harper was worried. Ever since Franklin had contacted them about what Felix Moya was planning and he offered to help them bring him to justice, he had been working feverishly to make this operation happen.

Every contingency had been considered, or at least that was what his planners and advisors had informed him, and yet things had still gone tits up.

After speaking to Charley, his man on the ground as it were, he had decided for the backup team to go and secure her location.

This required his personal attention though, so he took out his phone once more and dialed another number.

"Get me the Gulfstream ready, I'm going to Miami," he said.

FAIRFAX AIRFIELD

Jack got out of the staff car loaned to him by Tony and climbed aboard the waiting plane.

It was a Gulfstream G550, one of the most luxurious private passenger jets ever made. Inside the passenger section, there were thickly padded single seats in cream-colored leather, which complemented the mahogany trim. It wasn't the first time he'd traveled in this plane, so he was quite used to it and didn't react like he had on his very first trip, like a schoolboy in wide-eyed wonder.

The flight crew was the same, seconded from the Royal Air Force to the Security Services and in particular to SI6, but seeing as how SI6 was no more, they had remained to serve in the new section. Section Zero, as Tony had explained it to him, was the new name for the old outfit. Same job, just a different name. According to Bennett, it would be a different approach to the same problems; Jack had other ideas. SI6 had always been the third option when dealing with terrorism. The first being diplomacy, which seldom ever worked, and the second being military action, which was always frowned upon because of the repercussions. The third option was to take the fight to the terrorists covertly, to fight fire with fire, as it were. It was an old analogy but an accurate one, for many of the methods employed were similar to those used by the terrorists themselves. Some would argue that it was the only language they understood, but whatever the moral ambiguities of it were, this action produced results. In plain language, it worked.

As all this ran through his mind as he evaluated his present position, one thing came to the forefront, a tingle of excitement.

Before every mission, he used to get the adrenaline

rush of expected action, the impending danger of what was to come. Sitting in the comfort of this private jet, he experienced the same.

It could only mean one thing. Everyone had been right about him, and he was just too blind to see it. He had allowed his feelings for Melissa, his wife, to cloud what he knew himself to be true. Deep down, he was a soldier, a good one. He enjoyed his job and everything that came with it, not the killing, he accepted that as part of the package though. No one with a sane mind would enjoy taking another life, but there were occasions when there was simply no other choice. Not everyone could make that choice without severe consequences to their psyche. He just happened to be one of the few people in the world with the mental ability to compart-mentalize such events, to lock such trauma away until the mind could deal with it in a rational way so as not to cause harm to itself. He lived with the consequences of every life he took, every day of his life, he never forgot any of them, but somehow, he managed to live his life anyway, which was remarkable.

Post Traumatic Stress Injury was now a recognized illness that a lot of soldiers returning from combat had to deal with, but not only soldiers. Anyone who experienced a life-threatening situation was prone to this, and many more people were being diagnosed with it. For Jack to have been in this business as long as he had and to have not suffered, this disease was truly remarkable.

As the tingle of expected action coursed through him, he knew he was back doing what he did best.

Now to work though. He took out his phone and called Charley.

CHAPTER TWELVE

MIAMI SAFE HOUSE—AUGUST 23

"What do we do now?" Franklin asked again. Charley had lost count of the number of times he'd asked this question since they had been at the safe house, and the answer was always the same. Perhaps a different tack would work better.

"If you ask that one more time, I just may shoot you myself."

This seemed to work as he moved away and found a seat in the lounge, dropping into it like a moody teenager.

The problem was that she wasn't sure what was going to happen next. She was reliant on what Bill Harper was about to do, and she was having doubts about that too.

Who else knew about the meeting? Her only contact dealing with this operation had been Bill. It had been his decision to keep this isolated for security reasons. The Colombian Cartels were notorious for their ability to ferret out moles and their ruthlessness in dealing with them. Bill had argued that if they wanted to keep this op safe, then the fewer people who knew about it, the safer they would all be.

The safe house had surveillance cameras covering all angles from the outside, so from one single point inside, she had a three-hundred-and-sixty-degree view of the outside. If anyone approached, she would see them.

The safe house was also stocked with enough weapons to hold off an army should the worst happen, and she had a sudden feeling that the worst was about to happen.

In one of the screens, she saw two approaching vehicles. It was too soon for Harper's team to get here.

Who the hell were these guys?

She went to the armory cupboard and opened it up. Inside was a stack of assault rifles, LWRC M6A2, the standard assault rifle issued to the DEA. Made by the Land Warfare Resources Corporation, it was a competent and durable weapon capable of firing up to nine hundred rounds a minute. There were eight of them with enough magazines filled with the 5x56 cartridges to fight a small war. By the number of vehicles approaching, she thought she'd need all of it.

Franklin appeared at her shoulder.

"Shall I make us both a drink?" he asked. Then as she turned to see him, she saw his eyes fall on the screen and what was displayed there. His eyes went wide as fear distorted his features.

"Go and find some cover. This place is as secure as we can make it. Help is on its way, all we have to do is survive until they get here," she said as calmly as she could.

Franklin stood staring at the screen; fear rooted him to the spot.

"Doctor Franklin, you have to move, sir. Go find somewhere to hide and allow me to do my job." She eased him away from the screen and pushed him out of the room.

"In here is a safe room. Go inside and close the door. You'll be safe in there as entry is by a code that only I know. You can come out, but no one else can get in. You'll be perfectly safe in there," she reiterated, opening the large floor-to-ceiling door that looked like it could withstand an RPG blast.

Franklin entered the safe room and she closed the door behind him, securely locking it.

Turning from the door, she returned to the gun rack. On a shelf below the rifles were flak jackets, again, standard issue with the letters 'DEA' emblazoned across the back. She quickly threw one of these on, cinching the fasteners as tight as was comfortable. Then she took one of the assault rifles and, selecting a mag, she inserted it into the holder beneath and pulled back the charging handle to insert a round into the chamber. Picking up a few more mags, she walked over to the security monitors.

"Okay, you fuckers, bring it on," she said as she put her game face on. "Where are you Jack?" she said to herself.

———

Jack felt the altitude of the plane alter as it began its descent for Miami International Airport.

Sitting more upright, he fastened his seatbelt as the warning light came on. Flight Officer Warren appeared in the doorway, resplendent in her crisp uniform.

"Just checking on you, sir."

"I'm fine, thanks."

Just as she was about to duck back into her space between the passenger section and the flight crew cabin, Jack said, "Thanks again. Are you waiting to take me back?"

"Yes, sir, those are our orders."

"You know, there's no reason to be this formal all the time. I don't even know your first name."

"We're on duty, sir, so protocol dictates I use the proper form," she replied politely.

"I understand, but please call me Jack. I promise I won't tell if you don't. It can be our secret."

That at least earned him a smile.

"We'll be landing in a few minutes, sir," she said, then was gone through the doorway.

Well, at least I tried, he thought.

The plane taxied to a stop, and he grabbed his bag to leave.

"We'll be here waiting for you when you've finished, sir. Your car is waiting in parking lot number seven," Warren said as he went through the door.

"Thanks. I'll be in touch to let you know when I'll be coming back," he said, slightly disappointed that she was still using proper protocols.

"Come back safe, Jack."

Glancing over his shoulder, he smiled, "I'm surprised at you, Flight Officer Warren, not sticking to the proper protocol when on duty," he said with a wink.

She went back inside the plane, shaking her head at him. He was sure he heard her say, "You are such an arsehole," which made him smile even more.

He went over to the vehicle parked where she had said it would be and threw his bag on the passenger seat before climbing in. The keys were already in the dashboard, so he started up the engine with a push of a button and was pleased to hear the low rumble of the big four-liter engine in the Jeep SUV. He had the address from the phone call he'd made earlier to Charley on the plane, so he input the coordinates into the sat-nav. The destination came up with a travel time and destination arrival time of thirty-three minutes.

He steered the big SUV out of the parking lot and headed for the entrance to the airport.

Using the Bluetooth attachment in the Jeep, he called Charley. "I'm on my way to you, be there in around half an hour."

"I'm a bit busy at the moment, I've got company."

Jack heard gunfire over the line in the background and he pressed the accelerator to the floor.

She was in bad trouble, and he wasn't going to get there in time.

CHAPTER THIRTEEN

MIAMI SAFE HOUSE

The safe house was situated in an isolated location; there was only one road in or out, so Charley had an unobstructed view of the two vehicles that had approached.

The DEA had gone to great lengths to ensure this house lived up to its name by reinforcing the entire structure with steel. The instant she had identified the vehicles as a potential threat, she instigated the safety procedures.

Steel shutters dropped down, covering the windows and doors all around the building. The walls were reinforced with armor-plated steel thick enough to survive anything up to a .50cal shell. The interior electrics could be run on an internal generator, so even if the power lines were cut, they would have backup power. Finally, the building had its own self-contained air supply as the shutters sealed off the windows and doors. They also made an air-tight seal so that the houses couldn't be breached by a gas attack. It could last for up to three days which was more than long enough for help to arrive.

Charley looked at the men who had climbed out of the two SUVs as they fired their assault rifles at the house. A smile crept across her face as she saw the look on their faces at just how ineffective their bullets were.

Some of them peeled off to go around the sides of the house to see if there was any other way to breach this building which was all clearly visible on the security cameras.

As they all returned after several attempts at breaking in, the man in charge took out what appeared to be a phone. Placing it to his ear, he was clearly listening to a conversation taking place which did not require his involvement. This could only mean one thing, he was receiving instructions, which was borne out when his eyes went straight up to the camera lens. He was looking straight at her.

Seconds later, instructions were given. One of the men went to one of the vehicles and brought back an RPG-7.

"Holy shit!" she exclaimed.

Seconds later, she saw the leader point to the house, his men lifted their rifles, and the cameras started to go out.

The last one showed the leader standing there looking straight at her through the camera lens. He winked then the camera was shot out.

She was completely blind now and could only imagine what was happening outside.

The man holding the RPG-7 would be ordered to fire, which was confirmed ten seconds later when an enormous explosion rocked the building at the front as the armor-piercing round penetrated the door.

The safe house had been breached and was no longer safe.

Whoever had given those instructions over the phone had valuable intel on the security features of this safe house.

Before the cameras went down, she had seen at least eight men exit the two vehicles, which put the odds far too high for her to mount a successful defense of the building, especially as it had now been breached.

She had two options as she saw it. Option one, try to mount a defense and kill as many of the intruders as possible before they finally overrun this place and kill her, or option two, get inside the safe room with Franklin and wait them out.

Option one was a non-starter, for she didn't plan on dying today, and option two was not a viable one either. If they could breach this house, they most certainly could breach the safe room just as easily.

She was quickly running out of ideas.

Jack was still too far away to help, and Harper's team had been a no-show.

Picking up her assault rifle, she got ready to repel boarders.

She was upstairs on the first floor, at the front in the master bedroom, which was fed by a landing that ran around a balcony from a staircase that reached up from the hallway off the front door.

When that entry was breached, she heard men pour through the opening, going both left and right to clear all the downstairs rooms individually. It was clear they had training by how they moved. These were no normal bad guys sent by Moya to retrieve Franklin or silence him, this was different.

Footsteps pounded up the staircase, and she got ready.

There was a third option, but for that to work, she needed to survive the next few seconds and reach Franklin safely.

Taking a few deep breaths to steady herself, she burst into action.

Appearing at the top of the stairs, she fired a fast salvo into the first man she saw. The bullets shredded his chest as he danced with each impact, blood flying outwards in a red mist. He stumbled back to crash into the next man and him into the next.

The three of them fell back, dropping down and giving her a clear view of the others. She took aim and fired again, dropping two more.

Panic hit the rest of them like a tidal wave and they ran for cover.

This gave her the chance to move. As she ran, bullets chased her across the landing, peppering the wall as she ran from her door to where she had to go.

She slammed into the door, sending it crashing open. Beyond this lay the safe room and her charge, Franklin.

More bullets struck the doorway, ensuring she remained inside. She had no intention of leaving anyway, at least not by that route.

Stabbing the code into the locking door panel, she opened the door to the safe room.

Franklin stared out from inside the room, his eyes wide with fear.

"We have to move now," she said urgently.

"Why? What happened?" he asked, still rooted to the spot inside the room.

"No time to talk now. Just do as I say and move now," she argued.

Grudgingly he began to move, and he emerged from the confines of the safe room.

Charley grabbed him by the shoulder and pushed him to the side. There was another door there. At first, it looked like a bookcase set against the wall, but after moving the right combination of books out, it operated the locking mechanism. There was a loud 'click' as the lock disengaged, and the entire bookcase swung open on large, concealed hinges.

Before Franklin could comment his amazement, Charley pushed him through the opening.

"Stay there for just a few seconds until I make sure they're not following us," she said as she swung the door closed just enough to make it appear as if it had closed without the lock engaging again.

She returned to the door and peered out from the frame.

The intruders had gathered their courage enough to attempt climbing the stairs once more.

Another burst from her rifle soon put paid to that. Her salvo hit the first man she saw then she emptied the rest of her mag into the next in line. Stepping back around the doorframe, she quickly changed mags. A tug on the charging handle, and she was good to go again.

Stepping into the space at the top of the stairs, she emptied this new mag as she strafed across the stairs, killing two more. As the gun emptied, she returned quickly to the room and opened the hidden passage, closing and locking it firmly behind her.

The passage was dimly lit with overhead strip lights embedded in the ceiling, which gave them just enough to see where they were going.

"This way," she said, squeezing past Franklin in the claustrophobic passage.

"Will they follow us?" Franklin asked as she passed him by, his voice echoing in the passage.

"If you carry on shouting like that, they will, you moron," she chided softly, her voice like the hiss of a snake. Franklin tried to make himself look smaller by sinking his head into his shoulders in a completely unconscious move.

"Follow me and keep the noise down."

They continued moving down the passage quietly until she pulled them up to a stop. There was another door in front of them. This one had an electronic locking panel placed at the side, like the one that secured the safe room. Once she had input the correct code, the door unlocked, and she could push it slowly open.

With her gun at her shoulder, ready to fire, she moved out.

CHAPTER FOURTEEN

Jack saw the safe house in the distance along with the two SUVs parked in front.

The long driveway up to the house was the only way in or out, so he had them trapped. The only downside to this was that they outnumbered him by God knew how many.

Charley was in trouble though, and he wouldn't let her down.

There was no sign of life around the house, which meant one of two things, either everyone was dead, or they were all inside. It was probably the second one, as the two vehicles were still parked out front. If they had succeeded, then they would have left. He couldn't see any scenario where they all died, which meant the action was still ongoing and it was happening inside the not-so-safe house.

As he got closer, he could see where the breach had occurred. It looked as if they had come prepared and used explosives to gain access.

From experience, he knew these safe houses were
fortified in many ways depending on which three-letter
agency you worked for. Each one had its own identity
and specific methods of ensuring anyone inside was kept
safe. But this one looked as if it had been in a war and,
from his first glance, looked as if whoever attacked had
specific knowledge of where to hit and just how hard.

That smacked of an inside job.

Charley was in more trouble than she realized.

He pulled up the car as close to the other SUVs, then
got out, his Walther out and ready to fire. He approached
the building and entered through the hole that had been
blasted through the front door.

The first thing he saw were the dead bodies of the
men she had killed. He scanned the area for further signs
of what had occurred here. Bullet hits scarred the walls
and furniture, with spent casings littering the floor
underfoot. It was clear a raging gun battle had taken
place in this very spot, but there was no sign of Charley
or the man she was supposed to be protecting.

The SUVs were still parked outside, so they hadn't
captured them and taken them away, that left only one
other option.

They were still here.

Carefully he threaded his way through the building
following the carnage. His Walther tracked before him as
he was ready to fire on anything that proposed a threat.

From the way the bodies lay, it seemed that they
tracked her upstairs to one of the bedrooms.

Slowly, aware that time was not on his side, he
started up the stairs carefully and softly, placing his feet
on each riser, hoping they didn't creak and give his position away.

At the top of the landing, he looked at the walls.

Bullet holes seemed to track across the walls leading into one of the bedrooms.

That must've been where she made her stand.

Bursting into the room, he tracked across it with his Walther, but there was no sign of Charley or any of the men who belonged in those SUVs parked outside.

Where the hell are you Charley?

———

"Don't you move, girly, or I may have to shoot you where you stand," a voice said off to Charley's left side.

She had pushed open the door and gingerly stepped out from the dark interior of the tunnel, only to be stopped dead in her tracks by the sound of that voice.

A cold hard metal tube was pressed to the side of her neck as she went to turn.

"Nah, ahh! You stay right where you are, girly," the voice said again. There was no trace of panic or fear in that voice. It was clearly someone used to getting their own way.

A hand reached out from her opposite side grabbing her rifle and slowly relieving her of it. All the while, the gun barrel was pressed into her neck, letting her know what would happen should she try something stupid.

"You can come out now, Doctor Franklin," the voice said, inviting her charge to come forward from the safety of the tunnel.

Not daring to move, she felt the gun barrel urge her forward with a little gentle pressure as Franklin had room to come out from the tunnel also.

Slowly she took a step forward, followed by another, until she heard Franklin's labored breathing from behind as he fearfully stepped out into the light.

"What do you want?" she asked as her brain tried to come up with a plan. At the moment, she was at their mercy. She had, at the very least, three guns aimed at her if her calculations had been correct. She had kept count as the bodies had dropped from her shooting. According to her calculations, there should just be these three thugs left, which was no help to her at all. Not at the moment. She might as well have had a hundred guns aimed at her because it only took one shot from this range to end her.

"I have everything I want right here, little girly," he replied coldly confident.

From her peripheral vision, she could just make out where they all were. The one doing all the talking was off to her left, there was one to her right, but the third was walking slowly from her right toward her front. He held an assault rifle loosely in his hand, but the closer he got to looking her right in the eye, he brought the point of the barrel up to her face.

The talker was speaking again.

"I came to get Doctor Franklin, and now I have him. I don't need you anymore now, do I?"

The man in front brought up the assault rifle to aim at her. He peered around the sights to look her in the eye and winked, then returned his gaze back behind the sights.

Everything went into slow motion as time slowed down, stretching out the inevitable. She saw the shooter's finger go inside the trigger guard and start to squeeze the trigger.

She could count the rest of her life now in seconds.

Death on the job was always a possibility, but she never thought it would come this soon. She just wasn't ready to go, not yet. Not after meeting Jack Cross. It was then she realized, with everything else that was going on around her, that it was not getting to know him better that was most prevalent in her mind; at the moment of her impending death, her last thoughts would be of him.

She closed her eyes and then thought, *to hell with that. If I'm going to die, I want to look it in the eye.*

The finger tightened on the trigger, and she readied herself for the impact. It would be like a kick to the chest, her lungs would start to collapse from the impact as all her breath was forced from them, but the pain wouldn't come until later, when the shock hit her brain.

As the gun went off, she flinched, expecting to be knocked off her feet, but as she looked up, she saw the shooter's head distort as blood sprayed out to the side before he fell to the ground.

What the hell just happened? She wondered.

Another gunshot ripped through the air, and a second gunman dropped to the ground.

Someone else was shooting.

Reaching for her pistol, she brought it around to her left and shot the talker, who was looking around for this new addition to their little play. Her bullets hit him in the chest as he looked around. Confusion was evident on his face as his eyes dropped to the blood that bloomed on his shirt front. He staggered back and then looked up at her.

"Who sent you?" she snarled through gritted teeth.

"Go to hell, bitch," he replied. He brought his pistol up, placed the muzzle under his chin, and was about to fire.

Charley knew she had only one chance to find out who sent these guys, and he was it.

She couldn't let him shoot himself, but she couldn't reach him in time to stop him from pulling the trigger, so she did the only thing she could think of.

Taking aim, she quickly fired at his hand. The bullet hit his hand and went clean through, knocking the gun from his grasp, but its trajectory took it onwards. It slashed through his neck, severing his carotid. Blood spurted out in a thick stream, covering his front as he collapsed.

She was on him in a rush, dropping her pistol, clamping her hands to his neck, applying pressure, and trying to stem the flow. Blood pumped up through her fingers; as he looked up into her eyes, she saw the light go out from them, and he was gone.

"Shit!" she screamed, getting to her feet, her hands still dripping with the shooter's blood.

"Are you alright, Charley?" Jack Cross's voice shouted across the space between them.

She looked over to where he was walking quickly towards her, and she ran to meet him, throwing her arms around his neck and crushing him to her.

"You came, you saved me," her voice a husky whisper.

He gently held her away from him so he could look into her eyes, "You did say, next time, I'd get the drinks. You didn't think I'm the kind of guy to welch on something like that, did you?"

For a second, she wasn't sure if he was joking or not. His face was so serious.

"I had you for a minute there, didn't I?" he said, his face splitting with a wide grin, and she had to admit she'd fallen for it.

"Jackass," she said, punching him playfully on the arm.

"Come on, let's get the fuck out of here," he said, looking around. "Where's your man?"

Charley saw where he was looking and then scanned

everywhere around them. Peering back down the tunnel, she could find no trace of him there either.

Where the hell is he?

"I didn't see him back in the house, so I assumed he was here with you," Jack was saying, which brought another question to her mind.

"How the fuck did you know where to look for me, I mean here specifically, at the end of this exit tunnel?" she asked.

"What, do you think you Yanks are the only ones with safe houses that come with all the trimmings?" he replied. "When I couldn't see any trace of you up in the bedrooms, I noticed the bookcase and knew that was the entrance to the exit tunnel, so I just came outside to where I thought it would be. I admit that part was a bit of guesswork, and I almost missed you, but it all worked out in the end."

"Well, I'm very glad you didn't miss, well, them at least. It's all gonna be for nuthin' though if I can't find Franklin."

"Where do you think he's gone?"

"No idea, but he can't have gone far, no transport," she told him. It was then they both remembered the SUVs parked around the front. Sprinting around the side of the house, they were just in time to see one of the SUVs powering down the driveway.

"Come on, we can still catch him," Charley said, but Jack's hand on her arm restrained her.

She snapped an angry glance at him and was about to rebuke him when she noticed where his eyes had landed.

Franklin had somehow slashed the tires on all the vehicles, at least one per vehicle. There was no way they would catch him now.

He had escaped, but why?

Had this been his plan all along?

If so, then they had played right into his hands, and now he was gone, and they had no way of finding him.

"Holy crap, the honchos at head office are gonna chew my ass off for sure over this," Charley said.

CHAPTER FIFTEEN

Jack knocked on the door to Charley's room.

"Are you decent?"

Once they repaired one of the least damaged tires, they were able to drive away from the safe house before anyone arrived to see what had happened.

Charley had told him of the team her handler, Bill Harper, had sent not showing up, which raised alarm bells immediately in his mind. He chose not to voice his concerns though, until he knew more of what was going on.

They drove into the city and booked into a small hotel for the night while they considered their next move. After spending the evening eating a fine meal in a restaurant close by, they returned to the hotel for a swift drink before retiring for the night in their separate rooms.

"I'm a lot of things, but I'm not sure decent is one a

them," she said with a smile as she opened the door to him.

"What say we grab some breakfast and discuss our next move?" Jack suggested.

"Good idea, I'm starving," she agreed.

They went downstairs into the dining hall and sat down. Looking around, Jack saw a buffet table against the wall with a large selection of food, and sitting next to it was a drinks dispenser.

"I'll grab the coffee, you grab a couple of plates of food," Charley said, getting up and walking over to the drinks machine.

Jack grabbed two plates and started to fill them both with a selection of bacon, sausages, eggs, mushrooms, and some bread.

"Where the fuck are the baked beans?" he muttered to himself as he looked at the pancakes piled high on a plate sitting next to a huge jug of maple syrup. "Disgusting," he said with a shudder. He returned to the table and placed a plate in front of Charley, who started eating immediately.

"I thought they had tea in this country as well as coffee," he said when he looked at the mug of black liquid she had placed by his plate.

"I thought you might need the caffeine this morning. We've probably got a busy day ahead of us," she replied with a mouthful of bacon and eggs. She looked at him as he started attacking his food with gusto.

"Can I ask you something?" she asked.

"Yep, go ahead."

"Why didn't you book us inta one room?"

Jack almost choked on his food.

"Excuse me?" he said with wide eyes.

"What's the matter? You think I'm too ugly to fuck?" she asked with a straight face.

Jack placed his knife and fork down, wiped his mouth on a napkin, then looked her in the eye.

"Wow! You were thinking about what to say really hard there for a moment, weren't ya?" she said, grinning widely.

"I'm just fuckin' with ya man, well not literally as ya know, separate rooms and all," she added, returning her attention to her food.

Jack breathed more easily then. He picked up his utensils and resumed eating.

After a pause, he said, "This is a mission, and I didn't want to complicate things."

"Good answer, bit slow, but good answer. I thought you were gonna tell me you were married or some shit like that."

"I was married. We had a daughter, but they were both shot in front of me. I buried them a few months back."

Charley looked up at him, and he knew she saw the pain there. Saying it had brought all the shock of seeing them killed in front of him back in a torrent of emotion.

Slamming his utensils down, he stood up, knocking his chair over, and stormed out.

Why had he told her like that? Had he wanted to hurt her, or was it his way of shutting her up? He had no idea; the words had just tumbled out of his mouth like logs rolling downhill after the ropes binding them had been cut.

The morning air hit him as he stepped out onto the pavement in front of the hotel. The sounds of the morning traffic filled the air as commuters went about their daily routine, oblivious to what he was going through.

He felt totally alone.

"Jack, I'm so sorry. I had no idea," Charley said as she came to stand next to him.

"I'm such a putz at times. You ask Mike, he'll tell ya. My mouth just runs away with me at times, and I get into all sorts a trouble."

"Like just now, you mean?" he said turning to look at her, a smile slowly spreading across his stern mouth.

"For the record, you are not too ugly to fuck either," he added, keeping a straight face.

She relaxed, "Well, that's a relief. You know, us girls have all sort's a hang-ups about our looks."

"C'mon, let's go finish our food off before some asshole takes our plates away," she suggested.

They returned to the dining hall, and as suspected, someone had removed their plates, thinking they had finished.

"Shit, let's start over. This time, what say I grab the food, and you grab the drinks?" Charley said.

Jack dutifully went to the drinks dispenser and poured himself a large mug of tea and a coffee for Charley. He added milk to his tea and two spoonsful of sugar, then returned to the table.

They continued their breakfast and were halfway through when Charley's phone rang.

She took it out, looked at the ID, and her expression hardened. Placing it on the table, she said, "Go ahead, Bill, you're on speaker."

Jack knew she had done that so he could listen in on the conversation. No one else was within earshot of them, so it had been safe to do so.

"Where the hell are you, Charley?" Bill Harper's voice

came through loud and clear, along with the anger he was obviously feeling.

"I could ask you the same question, Bill. What happened to the backup you were supposed to be sending last night?"

"Who's there with you?" Harper asked, evading that last question.

"That's suspicious, Bill, evading my question like that. What am I supposed to think now then? What's going on, Bill? I have the right to know," Charley said, also evading his question.

"When my team arrived, all they saw was a load of dead bodies, one SUV with slashed tires, and no sign of you or Franklin. What the hell happened, Charley, and where the hell is Franklin?" Harper asked finally.

"We were compromised. Someone sent a hit team to capture Franklin. It must've been Moya, except that these were Americans, not Hispanic," she explained, leaving out the part where Franklin had ditched her and Jack coming to help.

"So why did you leave?" Harper asked.

"I deemed it unsafe to remain behind after the attack. The building had been compromised, and I had no idea when your team was going to arrive. Why did you send a team from DC?"

"I didn't. I used locals," Harper said quickly, then went quiet.

"I relocated to somewhere I deemed safe. I'll check in later with an update," she said and hung up. She stripped her phone and snapped the sim card, putting the pieces in her pocket.

"What're you thinking?" Jack asked. He had his own ideas but waited to see if she was on the same page.

"I think he sent a team alright; he admitted to using

locals. I think the team he sent was sent to kill us though, and not as he said, our backup," she explained angrily.

"I had the same thought."

"If that's the case, then this call was to find out if I was still in possession of my phone because they are tracking it to try and find both me and Doctor Franklin."

"Then it's time to move," Jack said, getting to his feet.

"Where do you suggest?"

"We'll know a bit more after I make a call to my boss and give him a sit-rep," Jack said. "In the meantime, go grab your things and we'll meet in the lobby."

CHAPTER SIXTEEN

MIAMI

Bill Harper looked at the phone in his hand as the call ended. He tried to reconnect the call but got nothing but a recorded message telling him his call couldn't be connected at this time and to try later.

He was sitting in a Mercedes SUV in the back seat next to a young operative who was working on a special laptop. He was logged into the network of satellites covering this part of the country, searching for her GPS signal. In the front were two more operatives, both hard-looking individuals.

"We lost her, sir," James 'Jimmy' Larson reported sitting next to him.

"No shit, Sherlock," Harper snapped back angrily. Putting away his phone, he looked at the young ginger-haired operative and said, "Give me her last location, we'll see if we can pick up her trail there."

"Hotel Splendide, just off Main Street," Jimmy Larson told him.

Tapping the back of the seat in front of him, Harper told the driver, "Okay, you heard him, let's go."

———

Jack and Charley drove to the airport where he had left the Gulfstream. Once they had boarded, Jack instructed the pilot to take off and return to London.

Jack watched Charley as she entered the passenger cabin and looked around.

"You look suitably impressed, don't worry, this isn't mine. I'm not a closet rich guy. This is strictly for work-related use," he said as he sat down.

Flight Officer Warren appeared in the doorway and said, "Can I get you anything to drink, sir?"

"I'll have a Scotch on the rocks, please," Jack replied.

"Make that two, darlin'," Charley added, looking at the young Flight Officer. When she returned her gaze to Jack, she was smiling.

"What?" he asked, a little confused.

"You have a secret admirer, Jack."

"It's no secret, Charley, I know you like me," he said with a straight face.

"You asshole, not me, her."

"It's against company policy to fraternize with members of the force, thought you knew that."

"You could at least smile at her," she said, then looked away, and Jack knew their drinks had arrived.

"Here you are, sir and miss. Macallan on the rocks," Warren said as she offered them both their drinks.

Jack saw Charley's eyes go just a little wider in surprise at the mention of the brand of Scotch.

"Ah, the privileges of wealth," she said, taking the

tumbler. Before Jack could comment, she asked, "Where are we going, by the way?"

"Back to my place."

"You'll have to buy me more than just one drink if you want me to go back to yours. Dinner at least, I would've thought. I'm not easy, you know," she joked.

"Are you always this flippant?"

"Life's too short, especially in this business. Grab it by the balls and enjoy it while ya can, I say," she replied, putting a hand on his knee and giving it a squeeze. "You, of all people, should know that, Jack," she added, then tossed the drink back.

Jack didn't know what to say to that. He had gone through more than some, more than most in his life, but he wasn't ready just yet to toss their memory away on a fling.

"Shit, I'm sorry, Jack. I shouldn't have said that. I was completely out of line. I'll shut the fuck up now."

"That's the most sensible thing you've said today," he replied. He got up and went to sit away from her.

He stared out the window, slowly drinking his Scotch, lost in his memories, pain etched across his face.

———

Bill Harper got out of the Mercedes and went into the hotel lobby. He walked up to the reception desk where a young woman was working. Turning on the charm, he said, "Good day, darlin'. Do you recognize this woman by any chance?"

She returned his smile and looked at the photo on his phone.

"Yes, sir, she and another man stayed overnight. They checked out just after breakfast."

"I don't suppose she left a forwarding address, did she?"

"I'm afraid not, sir. Is there anything else I can help you with today?"

"No, thank you, you've been extremely helpful," he said and turned to leave with the rest of his men.

"Where to now, boss?" Jimmy asked as they got back into the SUV.

Angrily Harper said, "Back to the airport, there's no way to trace her now. At least we know she still has Franklin with her."

"How so?" Larson asked.

"Didn't you hear the receptionist? There were two of them staying here, Parker and a man. Who else could it be but Franklin?" Harper argued.

"Are you sure about that?"

"What're you getting' at, Jimmy?"

"You said it yourself. All those dead bodies left at the safe house. Do you honestly think she's that good an agent to take them all out and escape? Even if you consider that to be true, why did she slash all the tires on the vehicles? She'd already killed everyone there. No one was left to follow her, so why go to all that trouble of slashing the tires?" Larson postulated.

Harper thought about it. Larson had made a good point.

"There was someone else there," he finally agreed. It was the only explanation. The slashing of tires was still a mystery though.

Why did she do that?

Larson said, "She never said Franklin was with her. What if he ran off after all the shooting started and slashed the tires so they couldn't follow him? The other guy at the hotel could've been whoever helped her with the team you sent."

That made even more sense, Harper realized.

"We need to get back to HQ. If your theory is correct, then whoever that guy was, his people are sure to make inquiries about what's going on. When that happens, we'll know for sure, and we'll also know who sent him," Harper said.

"What then, Boss," Larson asked.

"Then I issue a report that Agent Parker has gone rogue and killed several agents sent to bring her in. Any agency that sent someone to help her will distance themselves from her. They won't want to be involved in her situation anymore, so she'll be on her own, and that's when we get her," Harper said with a sly smile.

"What about Franklin?"

"Oh, we'll let Moya's boys find him. He'll soon turn up, and when he does, they'll nab him, and this'll all be over," Harper said as he sat back and relaxed for the first time since this operation went tits up.

CHAPTER SEVENTEEN

SECTION ZERO HQ, LONDON

The two of them exited the Gulfstream and got into the car that had been waiting for their arrival at Fairfax. Jack had called ahead to give Tony the sit-rep he had mentioned. The rest of the journey was completed in total silence, with neither of them even looking at the other.

The car took them to the underground car park, where they got out and walked the short distance to the elevator that took them up to the ground floor and the short walk to the office at the end.

There was no outer sanctum to this inner, as had been with the old SI6 HQ. Jennifer had a larger role to play now. She was in charge of comms and had a department to herself. Jack knocked and entered only after a voice inside had given permission.

The office was similar to the one Bainbridge had occupied when he had been in charge. Thick pile-carpet covered the floor, neutral colored walls were adorned with a few paintings of which Jack had no idea who the artist might have been. Jack was surprised to see Simon Bennett sitting behind the desk, which looked to be made of dark oak, sturdy and robust, on top of which sat a computer monitor with a keyboard attached. In the old days, several trays for the various files would be situated as the occupier would work through them. The days of pen and paper seemed to have gone forever. Everything was on a digital file stored in some database or on the cloud, somewhere where access could be granted for the price of a secure password.

Bennett was wearing a white shirt and red tie under a dark blazer and looked concerned, to say the least, as they entered.

"Come in and take a seat, you two. Glad to see you made it safely back, Jack," he said, indicating the two chairs placed before the desk.

"Thank you, sir. Nice to be back," Jack agreed. As he sat down, he said, "From your expression, I take it you found out something that I'm guessing is not good news?"

Bennett looked at Charley, assessing the woman, then turned his attention to Jack as he spoke. "It seems Miss Parker here has gone off the books with this recent mission, and those people she killed at the safe house were DEA agents sent to bring her in. That's the official report we're getting from DEA HQ in Arlington, at least."

"That's a crock of shit. This was a sanctioned mission that I've been working on for the past year," Charley blurted out.

Jack looked at her, not sure if she was telling the truth or not. Had he helped her escape from agents sent to bring her in or, like she had explained, had he helped her escape from someone trying to execute her to get to Doctor Franklin? Without further details and facts about this case, it was going to be impossible to learn the truth.

Why had Franklin run off? Had he panicked due to the attack on them and simply run off, or did he have his own agenda here? The truth behind this could only be corroborated when they found and questioned him.

Bennett was speaking again.

"Quite, and I tend to agree with you, Miss Parker. The report we got as soon as we started making inquiries about your recent activities seemed to be, shall we say, rushed. It was almost as if they were cobbling together something to cover up a mess they themselves had made."

"If you don't mind my asking, sir, who issued the report about Charley, er, Miss Parker?" Jack asked.

"It was issued by the agent in charge of the operation, Bill Harper, your handler I understand, Agent Parker," Bennett said.

"That is correct, sir, and thank you, and apologies for my outburst, it won't happen again."

"Understood, Agent Parker."

"That actually makes sense, sir. Bill was the only other person in the DEA who knew about my working with Doctor Franklin. Felix Moya has a reputation for recognizing agents we tried to implant within his organization, so he planned a long game. We found one of his men, Louis Sancho, and turned him, applied pressure so he would leak information to us. When we learned that a new chemist had been employed by Moya, we instructed Sancho to get close to him. Apparently, Franklin was a genius in his field, and Moya wanted something special made to stamp out his competitors. They applied pressure on him by kidnapping his daughter and turning her into a junkie. They threatened to let her suffer if he didn't comply with their demands. If he did what they wanted, they promised to get her clean, and the two of them could go on their way," Charley explained.

"Well, that didn't turn out quite as planned, did it?"

"No, sir, his daughter died from the drugs, she had a low tolerance for them and died through complications, or that's what he was told. I think they killed her to tie off any loose ends, to save any trouble of looking after her, and once he was working for Moya, there was no way out. They knew that, so they were a little lax with security looking after him. We made sure Sancho was the only one guarding him, and he sympathized with him, and that's how we got him to turn on Moya, by offering him a way out."

"What about Bill Harper? Where does he fit into this? Why would he say you've gone off the books on this?" Bennett asked.

"He liked to keep things close to his chest when working a case, and with this one, we knew Moya was paranoid about security, so we kept those in the know to an absolute minimum. There was Bill, me, and Sancho, and that was it. As soon as it went belly up, he was free to lay all the blame on me. If this had worked, he would have taken all the credit, obviously."

"Good old plausible deniability working at its finest," Jack commented.

Bennett asked, "Why do you think Franklin made a run for it?"

"It could be one of two things, sir. Either he was scared for his life, and when the bullets started flying, he just panicked and ran off at the first opportunity, or he has his own agenda about this," Charley offered.

"Any ideas what that agenda might be?" Bennett asked.

"None, sir."

Jack tried a different approach. "Any ideas what he was working on? You mentioned that Moya wanted something to wipe out his competition, any clue as to what that could be?"

Charley thought about that for a second as she gathered her thoughts. "We know he was a leading chemist, so perhaps he was working on a purer form of an existing drug, or maybe a new strain of something already on the street. I honestly have no idea."

"How would any of those wipe out his competition?" Jack asked.

"Where are you going with this, Jack?" Bennett asked, suspecting he had an idea.

"I'm not sure, sir, but if Moya wanted to wipe out his competitors, there are only a few ways to do that. One, you get their existing customers to go over to your brand by offering a cheaper product or better product for the same price, or you destroy your competitor's product forcing them out of business. There is, of course, a more direct method, and that's to use force and literally destroy your competitors," Jack said.

"None of those apply though," Bennett said.

"I know, sir, that's why I think something more is going on here. Without talking to Franklin, we can't be sure of anything," Jack said.

"That's why I want you two to find him and bring him here. The Drug Trade isn't just a US problem, it's a global one. So I'm tasking you, Jack, to assist Agent Parker here in her investigation into what happened. As far as I am aware, you two have not arrived here. So what you do from here on in is up to you. Liaise with Chief of Staff

Armstrong as to your needs, and I'll do what I can to keep the DEA off your backs. What I don't know, I can't tell them, right?"

"Plausible deniability at its finest," Jack commented again.

"Thank you, sir," Charley said.

"Have you anything to add, sir?" Jack asked.

"Just that reports came in of an attack on a villa in Colombia owned by Ruiz. There have been no survivors found yet. I understand he is one of the competitors you mentioned. The situation down there is getting out of hand, very close to an all-out shooting war between the Cartels. If that happens, it will destabilize the entire country. Their economy is run mostly on drug money the Cartels offer to the government as bribes to stay out of their business. If this dries up, then the country will go bankrupt, so we have to act fast on this one."

Charley looked down at her feet and looked uncomfortable.

"What is it?" Jack asked.

She looked up, straightened her back, and said, "It was Bill's idea to leak to Ruiz that Moya was producing some new kind of drug that would wipe out his competitors. As soon as Ruiz heard that, they attacked Moya's villa. His wife and son were both killed during the attack. We knew Moya would want revenge and would plan a counterattack. We saw that as an opportunity to get Franklin out of the compound. This is all our fault, sir. We caused all of this."

There was silence in the room as they took in what she had just told them.

Bennett was the first to speak.

"We are not here to point the finger of blame but to

deal with the consequences. Find Franklin, then we can see about putting all this right."

"Copy that, sir," Charley said.

"This is typical of your country's mindset. They think they have the right to meddle in the workings of other countries, other cultures, thinking that your way is the only way. How is that any different than the Islamic extremists you're fighting a war against?" Jack asked.

"Enough!" Bennett shouted before Charley could respond. Jack could tell his words had hurt her though, and now that he'd said them, he wasn't sure if it wasn't out of some need to hurt her after what she'd said on the plane or if it was just a strike against her government's policies.

Words were the one thing that once said could never be taken back. All he wanted to do now was move on.

Bennett said, "Agent Parker, you are not responsible for any of this, you were following orders set by your handler. If anyone is responsible, it is Harper. Now this is your chance to put things right."

"I'll do my best, sir," Charley replied, not looking at Jack.

CHAPTER EIGHTEEN

COLOMBIA

Felix Moya returned to his home after the attack on Ruiz's villa.

"Where is Franklin?" he asked as he got out of his SUV in front of his damaged home.

The man who met them looked afraid.

"Patron, we have a lead on him; he is in Miami, and the team is closing in on him. They await your order to strike," the man said.

Moya turned to the man next to him, the hulking brute who had been his bodyguard for years, "Quesada, I want you to go to Miami, take control of the team to ensure Franklin and Sancho are returned to me here. I will deal with them myself."

"Yes, my Patron," Quesada replied.

"Take my private jet and bring them back." Moya turned away and walked towards his home.

———

MIAMI

Franklin drove all the way into the city and left the SUV in a vacant parking lot in a mall.

He hailed a cab and had the driver take him to the airport, where he booked the first available flight out to New York. He didn't need a passport as it was an internal flight, and he knew he could get his at his apartment there.

He didn't have a phone as Moya had removed any method of communicating with the outside world when he had him working for him. While he waited to board his flight, he saw a shop that was selling mobile phones that were on a 'Pay-as-you-go' tariff, popularly known in the US as 'burner phones'. He quickly bought one and powered it up; he would need one if he were to success-fully escape from the clutches of the Cartel.

When his plan became known to Moya, he would tear the world apart in his haste to find him, so he had to disappear completely.

Once he had his passport, there was nothing to stop him from leaving the country and all of this behind him.

———

Sancho was running scared.

He knew what Moya was capable of, and he knew once Moya found out about him helping Franklin escape the villa, he would do everything in his considerable power to punish him. Basically, he was a dead man.

He knew someone who had a fishing boat, and he knew where he kept it. At this time of year, he would be busy taking charters out into the keys to fish for marlin and the occasional shark.

He drove up to the harbor where his friend berthed his boat. The *Lucky Lady* was the name he had given the boat in the hope it would be his ticket to the grand life. Many times, the two of them had talked, and his friend Manny Ortiz had wanted Luis to go into business with him as a full partner, but he had already been tied to Moya, and once that bond was made, it was almost impossible to break.

As he sat in the SUV, he could see his friend tie up the boat as he prepared to leave for the evening. He was probably going to eat in a local diner.

Sancho waited for Ortiz to leave, and when he was certain he wasn't coming straight back, he got out of the vehicle and walked towards the boat.

He knew his way around boats. He grew up near the harbor and, as a boy, had helped out with many of the local fishermen and occasionally with the sport fishermen who took out charters. He would act as cabin boy as the captain tended to the needs of his high-paying customers. Handling Ortiz's boat would be easy.

Untying the tenders, he threw the ropes onto the deck and then went up to the bridge. He knew Ortiz kept a spare key in a drawer beneath the steering column in case the main key got lost overboard while they were at sea. It was just a precaution. One he never had need of, but Sancho was glad of it. He inserted the key into the ignition and fired up the twin-throttle engine.

The tank was full. Ortiz must have refueled for a trip the next day, which also meant he wouldn't be returning to the boat tonight. This gave him some leeway on his escape. The alarm wouldn't be raised until the morning, when his friend returned to his boat to find it gone. By that time, he hoped to be well underway and far away from here and the goons working for the madman Felix Moya.

As he steered the boat out towards the open sea, he went through a mental checklist of the best place to go where Moya would never find him. The list was small as Moya's reach was long, and he would go wherever he had to for revenge on anyone who crossed him. Ticking off each destination as he came to them, he finally came to the one place where he was certain Moya would never think of looking for him.

Setting course, he set off toward his salvation.

CHAPTER NINETEEN

Quesada got out of the SUV he'd been traveling in. He had flown in from Colombia on a private jet along with his team of five men.

They had parked next to the SUV used by Sancho, and he went over to look at it.

Not far from where they were, he could see the ocean. He looked around. The harbor lights were coming on as the night closed in. The water in the harbor shone as the lights reflected off the surface, sparkling and dancing. Street lamps lined the edge of the walkway down to the harbor front.

Turning his attention back to the SUV, Quesada looked inside, searching for any sign of their quarry.

Nothing here.

"This is where Sancho grew up. It makes sense he'd come back here if he was trying to escape," he told the men.

As they gathered around him, he instructed them, "Go, knock on doors, learn something. Find out where he would go when he was down here."

He wandered off towards the dock, walking along it, checking out each boat moored there. They had all been brought in and safely moored for the night. When he came to an empty slot, he took out his phone.

"Nico, check out who owns the boat in pier twelve. Find out if he knows Sancho."

He walked to the end of the pier and looked out into the bay. Out in the distance, he could just make out a shape. It seemed to be moving away.

His phone rang, it was Nico. "Sir, the boat is the *Lucky Lady,* and it belongs to Manny Ortiz, a childhood friend of Sancho."

"Get the chopper ready, we're leaving now. He's taken the boat out, and if we're quick, we can catch him." Putting his phone away, he started walking back up the jetty to where they had left the SUV.

They had a chopper on standby at the airport; Moya had resources stashed everywhere, so it was just a matter of a quick phone call to access any of it.

Quesada stood, watching the harbor as he waited. Before long, he heard the sound of the chopper carried to them on the still air as the evening closed in. The lights of the aircraft illuminated the harbor as it came in to land, throwing everything into stark contrasts. The bright lights of the chopper threw incredibly dense shadows across the ground as it came nearer to the waiting group. As fast as it had landed, it was taking off once more as soon as Quesada and his men had jumped aboard.

"There's a small boat leaving the harbor heading out to sea. Her name is the *Lucky Lady*, find her now!" he told the pilot through the headset he quickly donned after strapping into the front passenger seat.

The chopper banked over and sped off over the jetty, powering its way over the sea and into the dark night.

———

NEW YORK

Franklin debarked from his flight at JFK and was through to the Arrivals hall. Moving fast, but not that fast to bring attention to himself, Franklin left the airport going straight to the nearest taxi rank.

It was the dead of night now, and all he wanted to do was sleep. He'd been on the go all day, running on reserves of nervous energy and numerous cups of coffee.

The taxi dropped him at his apartment, which he entered, turning off the alarm as soon as he entered through the door.

Everything was just as he'd left it all those months ago. A quick look around and he had the few things he needed for the next phase of his plan. His bags packed and ready to go, and with his passport in hand, he looked around, saying goodbye to his home for the past couple of decades.

A wave of fatigue washed over him, and he just wanted to lie down. He wouldn't get very far if he fell asleep on the run, so what the hell, he thought. Placing his suitcase down by the door, he walked to his bedroom. Throwing himself down on top of his bed, not even bothering to take off his clothes, he was asleep almost instantly.

CHAPTER TWENTY

AUGUST 26

Jack and Charley sat opposite each other in the Gulfstream as they flew over the Atlantic towards the United States.

"Where do you think he'll go?" Jack asked. It was the first time they had spoken since their disagreement in the HQ.

"He originates from New York," Charley said bluntly.

Without missing a beat, Jack said, "It probably makes sense then that he would eventually turn up there, especially if he left his passport at home and he wants to skip the country."

"If he wants to get as far away from Moya as possible, then he'd have ta skip the country," Charley agreed grudgingly.

"We'll clear things up in Miami first, then if we find no leads there, we'll move on to New York," Jack said thoughtfully.

"Why not go straight to New York? We could start at

his apartment and see if he's been there. It might give us a clue as to where he plans on going?" she said, offering a counterproposal.

Jack looked at her, she wasn't being merely argumentative, she was actually offering a viable theory.

"Makes sense. If he does plan on leaving the US, and so far everything he's done points us to that conclusion, then it would be a waste of time to go to Miami first," he agreed. He called the flight officer using the console on the armrest of his seat. When she appeared, he said, "There's been a change of plan, we need to divert to JFK."

"I'll inform the pilot, sir," Flight Officer Warren said, then disappeared back into her section.

Jack hesitated before he spoke next, he knew he had to clear the air between them if they ever had a chance of getting this working relationship back on track. "About my comment back in London, it wasn't directed at you personally, more at your country's interference over foreign policies."

For the first time in a while, she looked straight at him. "I suppose I knew that, Jack, but it still hurt. I suppose it hurt more because I knew you were right. I love my country, Jack, I would give my life to protect it, but there are times when I think we go too far in our pursuit for freedom."

"You know, someone once said to me that just because it's not a big deal to you doesn't mean it's not a big deal to someone else. We all look at things differently, from our own perspective, and if you apply that to other things, then the same logic still applies. Your country's quest to bring freedom to everyone may be skewed, and by that, I mean that not all cultures would embrace freedom like we in the West do. Your country thinks that everyone has the inalienable right to freedom, and you are right...but achieving it the way you want to, your method of bringing freedom to them goes directly against their culture. To embrace freedom, your idea of freedom, and everything it upholds is contrary to thousands of years of culture that is so ingrained in them that they know no other way of living. You are asking them to let go of their basic way of living, the way they have done things for generation after generation since the written word was first embraced, and for what, so they can have a Starbucks on every corner? Like I said, this isn't about you, I was just saying."

Charley looked at him as he spoke and listened. At no time throughout his little speech did she appear as if she would interrupt him. She just listened to what he was saying.

When he'd finished, she nodded. Clearly, she was thinking about what to say next. Jack wondered if this would turn into another argument and if he had made things worse. As he mulled over what he'd said, his thought was that he probably had.

When she was ready, she was calm and spoke softly, "We could get into a lengthy debate here about whose country had the worst track record on human rights issues and discuss which country had a broader impact on colonization and influence on the world as a whole, but we won't. We have a job to do, so let's just do it and move on. I'm not saying I agree with you or disagree. I'm just saying, for the moment, let's leave this conversation for when we can devote the time to go through it properly."

Jack nodded his agreement, and they went silent for a time.

This relationship would take some work. Jack knew they both realized that, and he just hoped their professionalism would come into play when the time was needed for decisive action to be taken and for them not to allow their personal issues to cloud their judgment. Neither of them would know until it came the time to act.

"It's been a long day, try and get some rest. We both need to be fresh when we arrive in New York because we'll need to hit the ground running. If Moya has sent anyone after Franklin, I doubt it'll be too long before they think to check his home in New York, so we need to be at our best," Jack said, turning in his seat to get comfortable. He rested his head against the backrest of the comfortable seat and was asleep in seconds.

CHAPTER TWENTY-ONE

MIAMI

Quesada peered through the side window of the chopper.

"Down there on your port side," he said to the pilot. Turning in his seat, he told his five-man team to get ready.

The chopper came over the *Lucky Lady* and hovered as the side door was slid open. The men were already strapped onto a drop line, and as the intense lights from beneath the chopper lit up the deck below, they were able to descend, one by one, onto the aft deck of the small boat.

Quesada was the last one to drop onto the deck, and by that time, his team had grabbed Sancho and brought him from the wheelhouse to stand with them on the aft deck.

Quesada looked down his nose at Sancho with nothing but contempt in his eyes. Sancho was not a small man by any means, he stood at a little over six feet and was physically fit, but against the brute Quesada, he looked positively frail by comparison.

"Why?" he asked simply.

Sancho was struck dumb with fear. Quesada noticed how he constantly rubbed his hands on his trouser legs to wipe away the sweat from his palms and how he swallowed as if his mouth had gone dry, all visible signs of fear.

Before Sancho could speak, Quesada asked, "Where is Franklin?"

Sancho shook his head, still unable to speak.

"Patron has no need of anyone who is useless to him. You, Sancho, are of no use if you cannot answer one simple question. So, think long and hard, and consider your next few words with the greatest of care because your life truly depends on them. Where is Franklin?" he repeated with menace.

Sancho suddenly found his voice as words came tumbling out of his mouth in an unending torrent.

"Franklin was with the DEA agent, a woman I was forced to work with, the last time I saw either of them. They were all at a safe house on the mainland when some other men came and started shooting. I had no idea who it was, but I saw my chance to leave, so I took it so I could return to Patron and tell him what they had forced me to do. When I got away, I realized no one would believe me, so I made it here and stole this boat."

Quesada just looked at him, and when he finally stopped talking, he stepped back as if he was getting a good look at him.

"So many words Sancho, but you still tell me nothing," leaning forward and putting emphasis on his last three words. They came out like daggers stabbing at Sancho's heart.

He saw the realization hit him, and all hope drained away as his face sagged. He knew what his fate was, and, in that moment, he knew he was a dead man.

Quesada took out his pistol, placed it on the forehead of the man standing in front of him, and fired.

The bullet tore through his skull, blowing out the back of his head in a shower of blood and brain tissue.

His men knew better than to stand behind his target. As soon as they saw him reach inside his jacket, they knew what was coming and moved to the side.

Sancho dropped to the deck, twitched once, then lay still, his life snuffed out like a candle flame in the wind.

Turning to Nico, he said, "Take this boat back and organize a clean-up crew to get rid of this," indicating the body, "then take charge of any follow-up here. You will be responsible for taking care of things here, do not let me down. Franklin had an apartment in New York. If the feds don't have him, then he'll have gone there. If he's making a run for it, he'll need his passport. We never had it when we took him, there was no need, so I am assuming it'll still be there."

"Yes, it will be done, Patron," Nico said with a slight bow.

Waving to the chopper, he indicated they were coming back up. His team grabbed onto the line and started the ascent. Quesada was the last to leave the boat, and when they were all back aboard, it peeled off and started its return flight to the shore.

As he sat in the front passenger seat once more, he isolated the radio and changed the frequency to one that Moya used exclusively. Once he made contact, he filled him in on the situation and what he intended to do next. Moya had given him a mission of finding Franklin and returning him to the villa to stand trial for his betrayal. He would not dare return empty-handed.

"Find him and bring him back. He is the only one who understands this new formula he has used. I see now I underestimated the man. I thought he was a beaten man, but clearly, he harbored resentment toward my treatment of him and his daughter. I want him back to ensure things are as he guaranteed to me they would be," Moya said.

"It will be done, my Patron," Quesada replied, returning the frequency to the normal one for the pilot.

It would take time for them to get to the airport and then fly to New York. He knew he could save time by getting a team to the address now to get hold of Franklin before he made his escape. Taking out his phone, he called a number of someone on Moya's payroll already stationed in New York.

Once the call was made, he looked at his phone, hoping they would be in time to prevent Franklin from getting away. The person he called would need backup should Franklin make a move to leave, so he called someone he knew could help.

———

NEW YORK

Detective First Grade Howard Patterson put away his phone and glanced around to see if anyone had overheard the conversation.

"Everything alright, Howie?" Ben Sharp, his partner, asked. Patterson's change of expression when he heard Quesada's voice on the phone must not have gone unnoticed as he thought.

"Yeah, everythin' is fine. I just have ta go take care of sumthin', ok?" he replied as he turned and walked off before his partner could argue that they were actually on a case and on duty. He knew Ben would have his back though, they had covered for each other through thick and thin over the past ten years that they had worked together. The last eight years of that working relationship, he'd kept a secret from his pal. A secret that, at times, burned a hole into his soul. For the past eight years, he'd been in the pocket of one of the biggest, most notorious Drug Cartel leaders this country had ever known, and all because he borrowed money to cover his gambling debt from the wrong people. Now Moya owned his debt, which meant he owned him as well. Any time Moya called, he had to jump or die. But of course, it wasn't just him...his wife and three kids were involved too, it didn't matter that they were no longer together and he only saw the kids on weekends. They would die just the same. It was how the Cartels maintained such an iron grip on their employees...through fear.

And he was afraid.

He left the scene and got into his car, which was parked nearby. He drove away, leaving the scene as fast as he could, observing all the correct speed regulations. The last thing he wanted was a speeding ticket, especially when he was somewhere he wasn't supposed to be in the first place.

It didn't take him too long to get to the address he had been given. He pulled up against the curb opposite. His instructions had been to see if the person who lived at the given address was at home and to call if they were. He was then to sit and wait for someone to arrive with further instructions.

According to the phone call, the apartment was on

the third floor. He left his car and crossed the street to enter the building.

There was a number pad on the front of the building. The owner would have the entry code to enable them to access the building. Patterson knew these buildings made the entry codes simple so the occupants would be able to remember it easily enough. He ran through the combinations he knew and struck it lucky on the fourth attempt.

He took the stairs up to the third floor. The door opened out onto a corridor that stretched out laterally in front of him. The door opposite him had the number eight at head height. The number he wanted was ten, so the apartment was over to his right. He turned, walked towards it, and placed his ear to the door to listen.

There was the sound of movement inside, so at least someone was home.

Leaving the apartment, he returned to the stairs and took them down to the ground floor again.

Inside his car, he took out his mobile phone and returned the call.

CHAPTER TWENTY-TWO

As Patterson was getting back in his car, Jack and Charley were arriving at the same address.

Jack got out of the taxi, and as he held the door open for Charley, he looked up at the building.

"This is where he lives, you're sure?" he asked.

"It's the address we have on record, yes."

"Okay, let's go," he said and headed off toward the entrance.

Jack noticed the keypad entrance lock. He took out his handkerchief, wrapped it around his finger, and started trying various combinations of numbers. Before long, he had hit the right code, and the door opened.

Saying nothing, Charley opened the door and walked inside. Jack glanced around one final time, then followed her inside.

———

Sitting across the street, Patterson saw the couple get out of the taxi and walk up to the entrance to the building.

Normally he wouldn't have thought anything was wrong, but there was something about how they carried themselves, the way they surveyed the immediate area as they got out of the taxi. These were pros, maybe Feds. Whoever they were, they weren't your average Joes, which spelled trouble for him.

He called that number once more.

"Two people have just got out of a taxi and went inside the building where I am right now, a man and a woman," he said.

"Why are you telling me this?" Quesada replied.

"Because the amount of time they took entering means they didn't have the code to get in, which means they don't live there. Also, they have that look about them."

"And what look is that?"

"The look of a professional going about their business."

"A man and a woman, you say?"

"Yes, why is that relevant?"

"It is none of your concern except to say that you are not to allow them to leave with the principal. Do I make myself clear?"

"Look, I don't even know who this principal guy is. I've never seen him, so I wouldn't recognize him if he walked right by me in the street. And one more thing, how do you know they are here to take your principal? They could just be visiting someone inside the building. I can't be certain of anything without more detail on what is going on here," Patterson said.

"I will send you a picture of the man I want you to keep an eye on. I have other resources in the area who will soon be there. If these two attempt to remove the principal from the building, you are to prevent it from happening. Is that clear?"

Patterson knew better than to argue with the voice on the phone. If he was who he thought it was, then he was Moya's right-hand man, and no one messed with that guy.

"Perfectly clear," he said finally.

"The people I called should be with you any moment. I have told them what you look like so they will announce themselves to you, and you will assist them in every way you can, need I say more?"

"No, I sit on my ass 'til your boys get here and do as they say, right?" Patterson said grudgingly.

This was turning out to be one hell of a day.

"Good, with luck, this will all be over soon, and you can return to your life," Quesada told him, then hung up the phone.

Patterson looked at the phone in his hand and thought, *If only!*

————

"You're sure this is the right apartment?" Jack asked as they stood outside apartment number ten.

"That's the number on his record, so yeh, this is the right apartment," Charley told him.

"Okay then, let's do this."

Standing to the side of the door, Jack knocked and said in the best mid-western American accent he could, "Excuse me, sir. I have a delivery for your neighbor, but they don't seem to be in. I was wondering if you would kindly take it in for them?"

He heard footsteps approach the door, and he nodded to Charley to get ready.

The door opened a crack, the man inside was about to say something, but Jack didn't give him the chance. He slammed his left shoulder against the door, forcing it open.

He was inside in a flash as he saw who he presumed was Franklin go staggering backward across the carpet. Charley followed him inside and came around him to confront the occupant of the room.

"Why the fuck did you run, Franklin?" she blurted out angrily.

"Because you were about to get us all killed. I saw my chance, so I took it," he replied, leaning against the worktop in his kitchen.

The door had opened out into a hallway that led into a kitchen area. Franklin had staggered back into that area where he now stood, staring wide-eyed at the two of them. To their right from the kitchen, the apartment opened out into the living space, where furniture was arranged neatly in front of a large TV screen mounted on the wall. On either side of the TV were two doors that Jack assumed would be the bedrooms.

Placed by the sofa was a leather travel grip.

"Going somewhere, Doctor?" he asked, cutting through the obvious tension in the room.

"Who's he?" Franklin asked, indicating Jack with a nod in his direction.

"A friend. Answer the question, Franklin, you goin' someplace?"

"Anywhere but here. As far from you and Moya as I possibly can," Franklin told her.

"You do realize he's sent people after you, don't you? He's not the type to let anyone get away," she said.

"That's why I didn't tell you where I was going."

"And yet we found you anyway," Jack commented.

Charley looked at him.

"They're probably here already," he said.

"The car across the street?" she questioned.

Jack nodded, he'd spotted it as they got out of the taxi, and he was glad she'd seen it too. It showed she was focused on the job and hadn't allowed her feelings to get in the way.

"Oh, Christ!" Franklin cried, slumping against the kitchen units.

Jack saw the fear destroy him. He wasn't an operative or soldier like them; he was just a normal man caught up in something he was totally unprepared for.

"Don't worry, Doctor, we're here to protect you," he said, reaching for his pistol. He jacked the slide to inject a round into the breach, then placed it back in his shoulder rig for the time being.

"We need transport to get back to the airport," he said, looking at her. "Any ideas?"

He saw her eyes light up. She most definitely had.

CHAPTER TWENTY-THREE

Patterson was jolted to full awareness by the knock on his side window. He was suddenly faced with someone staring at him, and then he became aware that his car was surrounded by three more pairs of glaring eyes, all focused on him.

Opening his door, he got outside and looked around him. These were the backup Quesada had sent to take charge.

His heart raced as he recognized the faces; these were people he'd had dealings with on a professional level. Their records had crossed his desk at Robbery Homicide at his precinct, so he knew not to mess with them. Out here on his own, he was sorely outnumbered and could quickly become just another statistic that would cross his or his partner's desk.

"Shit!" he muttered.

"Detective First Grade Patterson, how you doin'?" Max Givens said. He was a tall shaven-headed thug wanted on three counts of armed robbery and one count of attempted murder.

"Look, Max, let's just do this and move on 'eh?" Patterson said, wanting to get this over and done with as fast as he could. He was beginning to realize that his life was not his own anymore, and this was only going to get worse.

Givens flashed a toothy grin at Patterson, which resembled that of a shark more than a human.

"Okie dokie, Howie, let's do this," he said.

Patterson had remembered the code for the door, so entry when they crossed the street wasn't a problem.

"It's on the third floor," he said, and he held the door to the stairs open for them.

The four large men took out their pistols and proceeded to file through the door. Patterson grabbed Givens by the arm.

"What exactly are your instructions?" he asked.

Givens looked down at the arm.

"Howie, we're just going to grab the guy in apartment ten and hold him for Quesada. That's it, now are you with us or not?"

"I want no part of this," Patterson told him, backing off.

"You think you have a choice here, Howie? Get your ass through that door and up them stairs just like the rest a us," Givens snarled at him.

Patterson knew the only reason he had spoken to him like that was because he knew he was powerless here. There was absolutely fuck-all he could do to prevent this from happening. Givens was right, he had no choice, Moya owned his soul.

Patterson pushed past Givens and walked up to the stairs, then went up after the other three.

"This day just keeps getting worse," he muttered to himself as he ran up the stairs.

———

Jack opened the door and stepped out into the corridor.

"Hold it right there, bud, don't move," a voice said to his right then he felt the gun barrel pressed against the side of his face.

Before the gunman could do anything, Jack moved. He brought up his right hand, knocking the gun away before the gunman had time to react.

With his left hand, he grabbed the top of the gun and, moving fast, brought his elbow around and smashed it into the face of the gunman. He saw his shocked expression as his eyes went wide just before he was knocked out cold.

Ripping the gun from the unconscious fingers of the falling man Jack turned it on the next person he saw.

There was a group of four more large, tough-looking men coming his way, guns drawn. As the first one went down after his blow, the other four started firing. Bullets filled the corridor, forcing Jack to step back inside the apartment, slamming the door behind him.

"No way out that way," he said.

Bullet impacts were heard on the door, wall, and frame as the gunmen continued firing.

"This way," Jack said, rushing through the apartment to the bedroom.

"These buildings usually have fire escapes outside the windows in case of fire," he said, pulling the window up as far as it would go.

"You go first and give us cover from the ground, then you follow her, Franklin. I'll hold them off until you're both clear, then I'll follow on."

Charley nodded her compliance and threw her right leg over the windowsill and out onto the fire escape stairs. Jack watched as she scanned the floor below and the roof above for any signs of more gunmen. In the meantime, he watched the door, ready to act if they actually breached it before they could get Franklin free.

Throwing a quick glance out the window, he saw Charley making her way down the iron staircase.

"Right, down you go," he told Franklin.

The chemist dutifully followed Charley through the window and onto the fire escape.

Just as Franklin disappeared through the window, bullets peppered the door from the other side. The lock disintegrated under considerable firepower, and the door swung open, powered by a kick from one of the gunmen.

Jack was ready. Crouching down by the window, he waited for his shot.

Two men burst through the opening, going in opposite directions and covering the interior of the room.

Jack fired at the first one through the opening, his bullets striking him high on his chest, knocking him to the floor. The second man dived for cover on the floor.

Jack fired in his direction but missed the target. His two rounds struck the wall above where he had been seconds earlier, but they had the required effect. The gunman stayed down, giving Jack time to back out through the window.

"Move!" he shouted down the stairs to the two before him.

As he began running down the stairs, he kept an eye on the two people below and the window above.

A face appeared, peering over the lip of the windowsill. Jack already had his pistol aimed in that direction, so he fired two shots. The bullets struck the frame sending shards of wood up into the face just above, forcing it back inside.

Bullets pinged off the metal staircase all around him as he ran. He moved to the side, hoping not to get hit by a stray ricochet, then returned fire up at the shooters.

"Keep moving," he urged Franklin. Charley was already close to the ground and was getting ready to help provide cover for those following her.

Jack saw Franklin's wide-eyed stare as he looked up and then back toward the ground. He bolted frantically for the floor as bullets zinged off the metal structure all around him. He just hoped he didn't freeze or, worse still, make a dash for it like he did on Charley earlier.

Charley must've had the same thought because as soon as his feet hit the ground, she clamped a hand on his shoulder, roughly pulling him out of the line of fire.

Jack fired his last shots up towards the window to discourage any further involvement from those still inside the room.

He jumped the last couple of steps off the staircase onto the ground. He ejected the spent clip, letting it fall to the floor as he reached for a fresh one and slammed it up into the butt of the Walther, all in one smooth move. He jacked the slide on the move as bullets peppered the ground where they stood.

Charley looked up and returned fire until her clip, too, was empty.

"Take that, you fuckers," she snarled under her breath.

Looking around their surroundings, Jack noticed they were in an alley at the rear of the building. At either end of the alley were corners that ran around to the front of the building and the street outside.

"We need transport, and we won't find it here. We need to get to the street, there'll be a car there," he said.

He moved to the corner of the alley, and a bullet pinged off the wall right by his head.

Jack dodged back around, realizing what had happened. As they were making their way down the fire escape, some of the shooters had gone down the stairs inside the apartment block to blindside them.

Jack's face stung from where concrete chips had struck it.

"Try the other end," he instructed Charley. When he heard the bullets hitting the wall, he knew they were trapped.

"What do we do now?" screamed Franklin above the sound of gunfire.

Charley came forward and said, "What we do best, kick some ass."

Jack stifled a smirk, thinking, *Typical Yank!*

"I'll draw his fire, then you take him out," he said.

Charley gave him a nod and got ready at the edge of the wall.

Jack peered out and fired a couple of rounds toward the front of the building, allowing Charley to move out to the far end of the alley so she would have a clean shot at her target. The instant Jack stopped firing, the gunman appeared around the corner of the building about to return fire and saw the two of them waiting. Charley fired first, hitting him center mass with two well-placed rounds near his heart; Jack finished him off with a double tap to the head.

"Come on, it's clear now," Jack said to Franklin, grabbing him by the shoulder and dragging him along down the alley.

In his peripheral, he noticed a glance of approval from Charley when she commented on his marksmanship with, "Nice shooting," to give him clarity.

As a group, the three of them ran toward the front of the building, with Franklin safe between the two operatives. As they reached the street, Jack saw the final gunman across the front of the building at the other end of the alley. The shock of seeing them emerge from the opposite end was evident on his face by his wide-eyed stare.

Not thinking, just reacting to the situation, he quickly brought his pistol around to fire. Jack reacted first and shot him in the face.

The sound of the gunshot was lost amidst the traffic noise.

"There!" Jack pointed out. A vehicle was parked at the curb with the engine still running, and the driver was looking around, keeping an eye out for something.

"We'll take their car," he said, walking over to it and aiming his gun at the face of the driver.

Through the side window, Jack said, "Get out slowly now and keep your hands where I can see them."

The driver knew there was nothing he could do, so he complied. Opening the door and showing his hands to Jack and now Charley, who had joined him, he slowly got out. Jack noticed there was no trace of fear in the man's eyes. This was someone used to having a gun pointed at him. He was either a career criminal or he had military training, Jack deduced.

Keeping his gun on him the whole time, Jack instructed the other two to get in the car. Charley got behind the wheel, which was a good idea as she would know the area better than him.

As Jack kept his gun on the man on the curb, Charley was ready to go.

"What're you waiting for?" he asked, and Charley gunned the engine. Just before they drove off, the driver dropped his hands nonchalantly and then gave Jack a cheeky wink before they drove off, leaving him there.

Jack couldn't help but think that they had missed something. It was something that would later come back to bite both their backsides.

CHAPTER TWENTY-FOUR

COLOMBIA

Moya was getting impatient at not hearing about the capture and imminent return of his chief chemist, so he decided to take matters into his own hands.

Taking out his phone, he called Quesada.

"Why am I not hearing about you bringing Franklin back to me?" he asked almost petulantly in frustration.

Quesada's voice was guarded, which put him on edge. "Patron, I am waiting to hear from my team in New York. I dispatched them to capture Franklin and hold him until my arrival."

Moya looked at his Breitling watch, the diamonds on the bezel caught the light from overhead and shone brightly. A quick mental arithmetic problem later, and he had worked out Quesada's arrival time. "You should arrive within the hour, why have you not heard?"

"You know how these local boys get, Patron. They think they still have control of their territory. I have given them some latitude, but it seems I may have given them too much."

"Well, let them know who is in charge," Moya exploded as his anger burst over the rim of his control. "I want Franklin returned to me. I don't care what you have to do or who you have to kill, just get him here. The first test batch of the new drug is to be dispatched in twelve hours, and I need him here to supervise should something go wrong. Xavier, you know how much is riding on this. Get the chemist back here," he added more calmly.

"It will be done, my Patron," Quesada answered reverently.

Moya put away his phone and walked over to the drinks cabinet. His villa was undergoing severe restoration work after the attack, so for the time being, he was using the interior lounge as his living room. It was set at the back of the building, away from the driveway, and the only access to it was through the front of the building, past the kitchen, and towards the exterior swimming pool. Beyond that was his private helipad and garages, which housed all his expensive vehicles. He loved the trappings of wealth that his drug business had afforded him, and he had wanted his family to enjoy the benefits his hard work had provided, but that was not to be.

The drinks cabinet was by the far wall, and on top was a set of tumblers on a silver tray with a bottle of Macallan thirty-year-old Scotch Malt whisky. Slowly he picked up the bottle, twisted the top off, and poured himself a stiff measure of the amber liquid. Returning the top to the bottle, he placed it down on the tray and picked up his drink.

The smoky texture of the fine old Scotch slipped down his throat, and as the warmth began to spread from his stomach throughout him, he walked over to an armchair to sit down.

Running through his mind was his plan, the plan to rid his competitors of their customers by seducing them over to his superior product.

What if the plan was flawed though?

The plan itself was sound, he was sure of that, but what if Franklin had done something to sabotage it? How would he know? How could he find out?

There was only one way to be certain, and that was to force the answer out of Franklin himself. Only he would know the truth.

They had to find him, the plan was scheduled to start in twelve hours, and once it had started, there was nothing anyone could do to stop it.

He had to know the truth.

———

NEW YORK

"Where are we going now?" Franklin asked from the back seat of their stolen vehicle.

"More importantly, why did that thug smile at us when we drove off in his car?" Jack asked.

They'd been driving for about an hour and were getting close to their objective, JFK.

"Are we going to the airport? Won't they think of that and send someone to intercept?" Franklin asked when he saw the sign for JFK.

Charley stole a glance at Jack, he could tell she was trying to tune out the monotonous drone from the back seat.

"Shit, this car has a GPS. Of course it has. They've

been tracking us from the time we drove off," she said when it finally dawned on her.

"That's why the little shit was smiling. He knew exactly where we were going even before we did," Jack agreed.

"None of this will matter pretty soon anyway," muttered Franklin from the back seat.

Overhearing the comment, Jack turned to ask him, "And what's that supposed to mean?"

Franklin looked surprised he'd been overheard. It was a habit of his to talk quietly to himself in moments of stress or when he was in deep concentration. He ignored the question and looked away.

"Come on, Doc, what did you mean?" Jack persisted. He had some idea that this meant something important.

Franklin looked at him, and at first, he wasn't going to say anything, but this secret he was holding burned inside him, just itching to get free. When he spoke, the words came tumbling out in a torrent.

"It won't matter soon because I sabotaged the new drug Moya is planning on distributing freely by drone. He thinks it'll turn the existing addicts onto his new drug, but all it'll do is kill them all. Any addict already hooked on any drug being peddled on the market will be affected, and they'll all die. Moya thinks he's wiping out his competition by having them all addicted to his product and his product alone, but he's going to kill millions of addicts all over the world," he said, and he sat back suddenly relieved that it was out there.

Jack looked at him, and he was actually smiling.

"How is any of that even possible?" Jack asked.

Franklin was on a roll now and didn't mind talking. "Oh, the chemistry was quite simple, really. I was instructed to make a new strain of his new drug but to make it irresistible to existing addicts. He wasn't interested at the time in enlarging his market. He thought there were enough addicts out in the world already, and there was no need to turn the entire world into more, he just wanted all of them turned onto his product. I told him I could do that, and I actually began working on something that had potential, and then I learned they killed my daughter. I changed everything then. I told them that the old drug wouldn't last and a new one was needed. He believed everything I told him. He thought I was beaten, that he had total control over me. In truth, it was quite the opposite. I was in control. I developed a new drug that, when administered to existing addicts, would kill them within hours of exposure. Normal people would be immune to its effects, which was the hard part. I had to isolate the markers that enabled someone to become an addict in the first place. Those without those markers had natural immunity. After that, it was a simple task to mass produce it for distribution. He wanted to control the addict population, and I wanted revenge for killing my daughter. What better way than to strip him of his method of earning a living and turning him into a pariah in society at the same time, not to mention a mass murderer."

Jack shook his head in disbelief. "And when does this all start then?" he asked, glancing at Charley, who he knew was just as shocked as he was as she listened.

"In no more than twelve hours. The first batch is due for distribution over Miami. Once that is done, he has given orders that his drone fleet, placed in every country around the world, is to take flight and spray their load over the population. He plans on covering the world with his poison. I bet he thinks he's won. Instead, he's sealed his own fate," Franklin said.

"A drone fleet, you say?" Charley said.

"Yes, he got the idea from Amazon, actually. They have started to deliver parcels by drones, but he thought in broader strokes and bought a huge consignment of them and placed them around the world."

"We have to stop this," Jack said.

"You can't, it's too late," Franklin told him.

"I don't care, we have to try."

Charley suddenly made a sharp turn to her left, doubling back the way they had just come.

Jack looked at her and then all around them, wondering if she'd seen something to make her take evasive action.

Answering his unspoken question, she said, "I saw a gas station down this way a little while ago, it had a diner right next to it. We can change cars there."

"Sounds like a plan," Jack agreed.

———

Sure enough, there was the gas station, as she had said, and next to it with a car park in front and around the side was the diner she told him about.

She steered the car onto the car park and around the side parking at the farthest spot available. She got out, checking to see if there were any cameras watching them.

"Keep an eye out for anyone leaving the diner. I'll jack this one," she said.

Jack pushed Franklin against the side of the SUV she was working on and he kept a watch on the front of the diner while keeping a hand firmly against Franklin's chest so he didn't move.

She had the door open in a flash and was soon working on hotwiring the engine. There were a few newer models in the car park, but they all used keyless entry key fobs and were harder to hotwire. This was an older model which she had ticking over in seconds.

As he climbed in alongside her in the front, Jack asked, "Misspent youth, or did they teach you that at the DEA?"

With a smile, she said, "The former."

Franklin had been forced into the space behind the front two seats and was clearly uncomfortable and began to moan until Jack turned to stare at him.

He soon quietened down after that, and they drove off the car park and onto the freeway once more.

Jack reached for his phone and called London. He was put through to Tony in a second and was soon giving him a full sit-rep. Tony's reaction was the same as his own upon hearing the details of Franklin's scheme. "This is too important not to involve the boss in it. Hang on, and I'll patch him through," Tony said. A few moments later, Bennett came on the line after Tony had filled him in.

Bennett said, "You need to get to Miami fast and do what you can to prevent those drones from taking off and delivering their payload. In the meantime, I'll get onto the DEA and instruct them on what we've learned. I'll also contact the other security services around the world to be on the lookout for this drone army. We need their locations, so see if you can find a database that has them all listed. We have to get the authorities in the various countries alerted to this threat. Be warned though, Jack, until I can persuade the DEA otherwise, I'm afraid that Agent Parker is still a person of interest according to the report filed by her agent in charge, Bill Harper. It's clear he is covering his own backside over this, and he may even be complicit in Moya's operation as well, so the both of you tread extremely carefully. We can't afford any slip-ups at this late stage in the game."

"Copy that, sir," Jack replied.

"I don't have to tell you what's riding on this, Jack, millions of lives are at stake here, and we can't take for granted that Franklin's drug won't affect normal people either, so this has to be stopped. Good luck."

"Thank you, sir," he said and put his phone away.

"Well, you heard the man, so where to now then?" Jack asked softly.

"We need a way out of this city and away from Moya's reach. There's a small private airstrip we can use, the DEA has used it on occasion. If we turn up and don't give them time to check, we might just be able to persuade them to fly us out."

Jack's expression hardened as he said, "Persuasion is my specialty."

"I doubt that'll be necessary, Jack. Trust me, I got this," Charley said with barely a suppressed smile which left Jack wondering exactly what she meant by that.

CHAPTER TWENTY-FIVE

NEW YORK

Quesada arrived at the apartment building to find it surrounded by police vehicles and ambulances.

What the hell has happened? He thought as he instructed their driver to pull up at the first available spot at the curb.

As he watched the parade of police in and out of the building, he spotted someone he knew.

"Patterson, what the fuck happened?" he snarled through the phone when he saw him answer it.

He watched as the bent cop casually looked around the street, trying to spot if he could see the caller.

"You never said the person you wanted to keep an eye on had help. Who were they, Quesada, because they took out your entire team, including me, two of them permanently, and the other three were left holding their dicks, looking like complete assholes?" Patterson railed back at him.

Quesada was surprised at this. He knew Franklin had

help, he knew of one DEA agent helping him, but that was just a woman. She must have brought help along or met someone en route.

"Listen, Patterson, don't blame me for your own inadequacies. There was only one woman with him, you must be mistaken, or you fucked up," he replied.

"Tell that to the two men they killed, and it was no woman who took me out. I saw him clearly before he shut me down. He was good, I tell you. What have you got me mixed up with, Quesada? I deserve to know." he said.

I was right, she met someone, another agent perhaps. He thought.

"Why are there all these police around? I thought I told you to keep this quiet!" he demanded.

"By the time I came around, they were already here. Someone must've called it in after hearing the shots in the building, or it could've been after they killed one of your guys in the street outside. I don't know, I was out for the count at the time," he replied. "Listen, your boys have been taken in for questioning, so I suggest you get them a good lawyer. I'll try and do what I can from this end, but there's only so much I can do," he added.

"What about the man you were supposed to keep an eye on?"

"Before he was taken in, I had time to speak with your driver. Apparently, they took his car, but he told me it can be tracked by its GPS. That's all I can tell you. I have to go now. There's a lot of shit I have to clean up," Patterson said, then hung up.

Quesada told his driver to move off while he made another call.

"I want the tracking codes for a vehicle belonging to Max Givens. Send the GPS location to my phone," he said, then held it in his hand as he waited for the details to come through.

Within seconds he received a text with the coordinates of the car in it. He gave them to the driver, who inserted them into the car's sat-nav, and they were off.

He looked at the screen, which told him their arrival time.

"I want them caught," he said to the driver, who increased their speed accordingly.

Quesada wasn't afraid of getting stopped for speeding, firstly, they would have to catch them, and secondly, he had connections who could help intercept any charges being brought against them.

The need for speed was becoming more acute as things were beginning to spiral out of control, and he could see a monumental disaster rearing its head on the horizon.

———

Jack got out of the car as soon as Charley pulled up outside the small Control Tower.

The small flying club was a private, members-only affair that the DEA had on occasion used for local flights when organizing a commercial flight was not a viable proposition.

It was run by Woodrow Hagerty, an ex-Airforce pilot who took early retirement and set up this club. Combining his passion for flying with a commercial prospect, he had made a small fortune aiming the club at the one percent of society who could afford his fees. He also farmed out his services to other three-letter agencies, which brought in more than enough to live on by their fees alone.

By the way, Charley greeted the tall silver fox who met them as they got out of the car, Jack deduced she knew him pretty well, making her earlier comment finally clear.

The man was slim but fit. Even though he looked to be in his forties, Jack guessed his age was skirting more toward the latter stages of his fifth century. He had an infectious smile, and when he saw Charley, his whole face lit up.

Jack remained at the car, keeping an eye on Franklin while Charley said their 'hellos'.

There was a genuine affection between the two of them, evident in how they acted together. Hagerty seemed very tactile, always touching her hand or placing a hand on her hip or around her waist. Clearly, there was something, or had been something, between these two, and it had been close.

Charley waved them over.

"Woodie, this is Jack Cross, someone I'm working with from England. He's one a the good guys," she said, introducing him.

The tall pilot held out a hand in greeting and, with a warm smile, said, "Pleased ta meet ya, any friend a Charley's is a friend a mine."

"Nice to meet you too, Woodie," Jack replied, giving his hand a shake. He was pleased to find the man had a firm grip, and his palms were dry. The last thing he wanted to do was fly with a pilot who had sweaty palms. It did not bode well for their journey.

"We're transportin' Doctor Franklin here back to Miami, and we ran into a little difficulty," she was saying.

Jack saw that Franklin was about to add something, but he scowled at him, which made him think twice.

"You're in luck, baby girl, I just had one a my G550s

serviced this morning, and I was about to take her out for a test flight. I suppose we can take a detour and drop you off where ya wanna go," Woodie replied, still smiling. He seemed pleased to be able to spend a little more time with her and wasn't shy about showing it.

"We'd appreciate it very much if you could, Woodie. The thing is, we're runnin' late and need to get there like yestaday," she told him.

"Well, what a we standin' around here jabberin' on about for, let's get that baby airborne," Woodie replied with as much enthusiasm as he'd ever seen in anyone.

Jack was watching this bi-play and was quite impressed at the way she had worked him. To be honest though, he did seem quite the willing participant in all of this.

"Let's go," she mouthed at Jack as Woodie ran off to get the plane prepared.

"He seems nice," Jack said, which earned him a playful punch on the arm, confirming what he had already deduced.

"When you two have quite finished beating each other up, are any of you going to inform the good pilot just what you've dragged him into here?" Franklin asked.

Charley glanced at him, "He's in no danger. All he has to do is drop us off and leave. It's no biggie, he'll be outta there before anyone even knows he's been there."

"Time's running out on us. I just hope we can get there in time. We'll figure out what we're going to do to stop them once we hit the ground," Jack said.

"I've already told you, there's nothing you can do," Franklin butted in.

Jack gave him a steely glare, "We'll see about that."

CHAPTER TWENTY-SIX

Quesada's car rolled up to a stop close to the flying club gates.

"According to the sat-nav, Patron, Givens' car is parked over there," the driver said.

Quesada looked around, searching for any signs that who they were after was nearby.

"Go, find out where they went," he ordered the two men in the rear seats. They quickly got out and walked over to the Control Tower.

With the flying club being a small affair, there was no need for anyone to be there permanently. Flights could be logged into Air Traffic Control with a simple phone call on most occasions, especially with local and small flights.

Quesada watched as the two men entered the building but came back out almost immediately. Running back to the car, one of them said, "There's no one here, Patron. The place is empty."

"Well, they were here at some point and not too long ago because the car is still here. There's no way of knowing where they went either, not yet."

"What do you mean, Patron?" one of them asked.

Quesada's mind was whirring, trying to come up with a solution to this problem. He couldn't just return to Colombia without Franklin, not unless he'd attempted everything he could think of.

There was an idea forming in his mind. He took out his phone and called a number.

"Yes, hello, I'm trying to book a private flight from the Woodrow Hagerty Aero Club, but I don't seem to be able to get in touch with anyone there. Do you have a contact number for them, please? It really is rather urgent, and my client can be quite a bear if they don't get what they want," he said in his best servile manner.

He soon had what he needed and dialed the number, which was patched through to the plane Hagerty was on with Charley and Jack.

Hagerty answered through his headset, "Hello, Woodrow Hagerty speaking, how can I be of service?"

"I was looking to book a flight with your company, but there doesn't seem to be anyone here; when will the next flight be available?" Quesada asked.

"Well, I'm just ferrying a charter right now, sir. I won't be back for a few hours, but I do have other planes that will be available real soon. In fact, there should be one arriving there in the next half hour."

"That's a pity, I was hoping to book you personally. Where are you heading, if you don't mind my asking?"

"We're just off to Miami, so if you want me personally, sir, you will have a few more hours to wait before I can turn this little lady around and head back that way. My other pilots will take good care of you though, sir, you have my word on that," Hagerty assured him.

"Thank you, I'm sure they will," Quesada said, then hung up.

Turning to the others who had been listening, he said, "We need to find the next plane out and get back to Miami right away. I think I know where they're going."

———————

Jack and Charley were relaxing the best they could, knowing what was in store for them when they reached their destination.

Jack overheard part of the conversation from the pilot's cabin as the partition had been left open so Hagerty could chat to Charley during the flight. What he heard made him curious.

"Got another client, Woodie?" he asked.

"Yeah, when there's no one at the club, all calls get re-routed to me wherever I am, either in flight through a satellite link or through to my cell. Some rich dude wanted me personally to fly him or his client someplace," Hagerty replied.

"Did he mention where he wanted to go?" Jack asked, which brought Charley to full attention as she picked up on something too.

"Funnily enough, they didn't, but they did ask where I was taking you guys. You're not being chased or anything like that, are you, 'cause I went and told 'em where we're headed?" Hagerty said with a slight snigger.

Jack glanced at Charley, and he could see in her eyes she was thinking the same thing as him.

"Oh shit, you are, aren't you? Being chased, I mean?" Hagerty said when there was no response from them.

"We can't say too much, Woodie. Just know that what we're doin' is vitally important, and if those guys are who we think they are, it would be best they didn't get on your next flight," Charley said.

"I'll see what I can do to delay my guy that's due to land in the next half hour," Hagerty said.

"Thanks," she replied.

"We still have a bit of a headstart on them, but if they know we're headed for Miami, they could get someone to intercept us on arrival," Jack said.

Charley looked worried for the first time since he'd met her.

"This is something much bigger than I've ever handled, Jack, and I'm beginning to think I'm in way over my head," she admitted.

"I'll call my HQ and see if there's anything they can do on their end to help and to see what updates there've been in this whole situation," he said, hoping to ease the stress she was feeling. The last thing any of them needed was for one of them to buckle under the pressure.

CHAPTER TWENTY-SEVEN

COLOMBIA

Moya had waited long enough. Time was running out, and there had been no word from Quesada other than to say Franklin had gotten away from him.

This was not good enough, he had planned long and hard for this moment, and he was not going to allow anyone to tear it away from him.

He would go to the distribution site and await the arrival of his man.

Taking out his phone, he called Quesada.

"Where are you?" he demanded when his right hand answered.

"On my way back to Miami, Patron, I have reason to believe that the agent who took Doctor Franklin is returning to Miami. They are probably going to try and delay the distribution of the drugs."

Moya thought about that for a moment. Why would they try to delay the distribution? Wouldn't it be better for them to try and seize the shipment to use as evidence in a case against him? What else was going on here?

"Why would they do that?"

"I have no idea, Patron. I just know they are returning to Miami, and I can think of no other reason for them all to make the journey."

"Get back here as fast as you can, Quesada. Something is wrong, and I want to know what it is. I will meet you at the distribution site." Moya dialed another number, and when the call was answered, he said, "Get all the men you can spare and meet me at the front of the villa. We are going to ensure the safety of the shipment, so make sure they are all armed."

Grabbing his jacket, he walked towards the door. Whatever Franklin had done, he would make him pay with his life.

———

By the time the Gulfstream carrying Jack and Charley landed at Miami, the sun was going down fast.

Jack looked at the horizon as the sun dipped below it, casting everything in a vibrant orange glow. He turned to Franklin, seated across the aisle from him. "What time exactly is this shipment set for delivery?"

"Midnight, why?" replied the aging chemist.

Jack looked at Charley, who wore the same worried expression as him.

"That gives us less than three hours," she observed.

"I told you it was too late," Franklin said, looking away as if he was the adult trying to explain something to two disbelieving teenagers.

"Let's go, we have no time to waste," Jack urged as he got to his feet.

Franklin's head snapped around. "Why? Where're we going?"

"You're going to show us exactly where this shipment is while it awaits delivery," Jack explained.

"It's no use. It's at the docks, you'll never get to it. The security is airtight. Moya has men covering the entire docks. You won't get anywhere near it. It's too late, I tell you," Franklin argued, remaining in his seat.

Jack grabbed the older man by the collar and pulled him to his feet. He stared directly into his face as he said, "Why is it, Doctor, that you continually put up obstacles in front of us instead of helping us do our jobs? Don't you want to save all those lives?"

Franklin fought to free himself and then stormed off down the length of the plane.

"No, I don't. As far as I'm concerned, they can all go to hell," he shouted. "I made that strain of drug to do exactly that, to kill every last addict it touched. Don't you see, drug addiction is a plague that's slowly killing off humanity. All I've done is speed up the process, that's all."

"So, this isn't just about getting revenge on Moya then?" Charley offered.

"At first it was, yes. He killed my daughter and forced me to do things I never thought possible, but the longer I was in his grip, the more I got to think about the situation in general. He wanted to wipe out his competition by distributing a drug that would be so addictive all the addicts would turn to him for their supply. No other dealers would be able to supply them with what they craved, what they needed just to function as normal human beings, but then I thought I could kill two birds, as it were. I could destroy both his competitors as well as his own business by killing off all the addicts in the world. No more addicts, no more need for his drugs. It was a win, win situation all around. I would not only rid the world of this plague but destroy all the dealers in the world in one fell swoop, not to mention helping out with one of this planet's largest problems, overpopulation."

Jack glanced at Charley, were they both hearing the same thing here?

"You're quite mad, Doctor. You do realize that, don't you?" he said finally after everything he had said sank in.

Franklin looked from one to the other, his expression of confusion widening his eyes.

"Am I?" he asked honestly.

"Okay, Doc, you said the delivery was to be completed by drones. Just how did this come about?" Charley asked, trying to change the topic yet stay on point and learn as much as they could about this whole thing.

"Moya wanted to give the drug away for free, the first sample at least. After that, he thought they would all come clambering to him for their next dose. I decided to make this a one-shot deal, get it done all at once," Franklin explained.

"So what? You were just going to have the drones deliver the drugs to every addict? How, Doc? How would you get to every addict?" Jack asked. He couldn't see how they would work out all the logistics for something as complex as this, but when he saw the smile spread across Franklin's face, it dawned on him.

"Oh shit, now I get it. The drugs are aerosolized! You were going to spray the entire population of Miami with your drugs."

Franklin slowly nodded his head.

"Quite simple when you think about it," he said with a satisfied grin.

"What about those innocents who might have an allergic reaction to your drugs?" Charley asked, furious at him.

"More importantly, how do you know only addicts will be affected, and how does it target just addicts anyway?" Jack asked clinically. His mind was still trying to process all the information about this wild scheme of Franklin's.

"That was a little harder. I had to target opioids so that it would recognize the drugs that addicts rely on for their fix. Anyone with an opioid addiction would be a target."

Jack leaned forward, grabbed the Doctor again, and brought him close to his face once more.

"But what about all the prescription drugs that have an opioid base? There are many people taking strong painkillers that have some opioid component, such as fentanyl, or cancer patients on morphine. Your drug will target all those innocents as well. You'll kill thousands more, Doctor," he snarled angrily directly into his face.

He watched as the realization washed over his face about all the deaths, innocent deaths, he was about to cause.

"You may have wanted to rid the planet of all those addicts, Doctor, who you saw as a blight on humanity, but what about the rest 'eh? Are you okay with causing their deaths as well?" Jack asked as he released his hold on the chemist.

Franklin sank to his knees as he placed his hands over his face. Jack saw his shoulders shake, and he heard the cries of anguish and grief as he sobbed with the realization of what he'd done.

"You can still stop this, Doctor; help us to stop this delivery from going out," Jack pleaded.

When Franklin looked up, his face was smeared with tears running down his face. Jack saw the anguish in his tired eyes as the strain of the past months finally caught up with him, and what he'd done hit home. Before that, he had managed to block off what he planned from the side of his brain that housed his moral compass, where his ethics resided. Somehow Jack knew that all of that had just been released to see the light of day, and it had overwhelmed him.

"Of course, what do you want of me?" he asked.

CHAPTER TWENTY-EIGHT

PORT MIAMI—AUGUST 26

PortMiami is a major seaport located in Biscayne Bay, Miami, Florida. It is the largest passenger port in the world and one of the largest cargo ports in the United States of America.

Formally known as the Dante B Fascell Port of Miami, it is located on Dodge Island, which is a culmination of three historic islands, Dodge, Lummus, and Sam's Island. They have been combined into one and was named in honor of nineteenth-term Congressman Dante Fascell. It is connected to Downtown Miami by Port Boulevard, a causeway over the Intracoastal Waterway.

As Moya arrived, he had his driver take him to the cargo section reserved for his containers.

He got out of the car and was greeted by Quesada.

"How did you get here so fast?" he asked when his right-hand man strode over to him.

"I pulled a few strings, Patron, and got here as fast as

I could; a direct flight on a private charter and then a chopper to here," Quesada replied.

"Any sign of Franklin yet?" Moya asked, placing a grateful hand on his soldier's shoulder.

"Not yet, Patron, but when he gets here, we will be ready," Quesada said with an angry snarl that savagely curled his lip.

"Good. In the meantime, we will continue with the delivery of the shipment," Moya said.

———

Jack, Charley, and Franklin had landed at the airport and hired an SUV as soon as they got off the plane. Franklin was put in the rear seat again as they drove out of the airport.

"Put your foot down if you want to get there before the drones are released," Franklin said from the back seat.

Jack glanced at Charley, who had taken over the driving chores once more, and said with a smile, "You heard the man, move it, lady." Even in the direst of situations, soldiers had the knack of finding humor.

Charley kept her comments to herself and slammed her foot down hard on the accelerator pedal.

Jack glanced at his watch.

"How long have we got?" Charley asked without looking at him.

"Not long enough."

"How will we find where the drones are kept? Port-Miami is a vast place, it'll take us forever if we have to search it all." Jack asked.

"Especially with just the two of us," added Charley.

"You'll know," was all Franklin would admit from the back seat.

Jack and Charley exchanged knowing glances that said they hoped he was right or this could take forever. The port security would be alerted to their presence pretty soon after their arrival, and if the alert for Charley was still active, they could have the feds to deal with as well, so no pressure then.

The rest of the journey was completed in silence, with sounds of quiet snoring emanating from the back seat as the good doctor even managed to grab a little shut-eye during that time.

"Here we are," Charley said softly as they approached the area.

"What now?" Jack asked as he looked around for a way in.

Normally he would call on his overwatch, who would be relaying data from a satellite view through his comms so that he had a better picture of the area, all the entrances, exits, where the guard stations were located, and if there were any guards patrolling the area, but this time he was truly on his own. The only resource he had at his disposal was the DEA agent at his side, Charley Parker.

"Moya has his own entrance around the cargo section. He made a deal with the port authorities to allow him access whenever he wanted. We could try there," Franklin offered from the rear cabin.

Jack glanced at Charley and, with a shrug, said, "Worth a try."

"What do we do about him?" she asked with a nod toward the back of the SUV.

Jack looked at the chemist assessing him.

"Is there anything we need to know about this drug

before we go in there? How do we neutralize it if we can't prevent the drones from taking off?" he asked.

"You can't. Once they are airborne, the drones are programmed to release the drug over the most populated areas. All the drones are guided by a computer program that is installed into their software and is controlled by a central console. Once the code is entered into that console, the program begins, and there is no turning back. There is no kill switch, no way to reprogram them, and no way to stop them."

Franklin hung his head in shame after delivering those words, adding two more, "I'm sorry."

Jack looked at Charley, who wore the expression he was sure he mirrored.

What could they do? How could they stop this?

"We'll just have to destroy the drones before they take off then," he said, seeing no other solution.

"You said that Miami was to be the first, a sort of testing ground," Jack said, turning back to Franklin.

"Yes, that's correct. When he saw how this turned out, he was going to issue the order to distribute all the rest. He has distribution centers similar to this, filled with automatic drones on the same program over every major city in the United States. Once he had conquered his home turf, he planned on going international."

"Get on to the authorities with the locations of every other distribution center and let them know what they're dealing with. Also let them know how to destroy the drones."

"They'll never believe me, they'll consider it nothing more than a crank call," Franklin argued.

"He's right, Jack, they'll never believe him," Charley agreed.

Jack thought about it for a second, and there was only one other way.

Taking out his phone, he called HQ.

When the call was answered, he said, "Director Bennett, I have someone here you need to listen to." Jack handed his phone to Franklin.

"Tell him everything."

CHAPTER TWENTY-NINE

PORT MIAMI—AUGUST 26

The dock lights illuminated the entire area, the intense lights casting long shadows over where the containers reached up to the night-sky like inanimate sentinels guarding some hidden treasure.

Two figures crouching low flitted from shadow to shadow as they wound their way to the entrance reserved for Moya and his men. The gates were open, but there was a pair of armed guards watching it, their assault rifles held at high-port, ready to move to firing position at a moment's notice.

Jack looked down from where they had parked above the entrance and glanced at Charley. "There has to be another way in than through there. The moment we even approach, they'll know we're here, and even if we could get through that gate, it would take them, what, thirty seconds or so to hunt us down."

He saw Charley look around, also assessing their situation.

Turning back to him, she smiled, "What we need is a diversion."

———

Moya entered the small room overlooking the dock area. It was from here that most of the operations were overseen. It was also from here that the computer-controlled drones would receive the signal to start the delivery.

"What had Franklin done that would make him come back here?" He asked no one in particular. This question had been rattling around inside his mind since the chemist had made a run for it. Had he somehow sabotaged this whole operation? He could see no way that he could do that. Everything had been checked and double-checked. The drug had been manufactured to his formula and deposited inside the drones for aerial release. There was no way he could have tampered with anything. The only thing that had been under his control had been the drug, the formula had been his and his alone, and he had guaranteed it would work. He had sworn on his life that every addict it touched would want more, and only his drug would satisfy their needs. Every addict in the country would turn to him for their product. It was infallible. He had won. All that needed to be done was deliver the drugs.

Still, there was something that nagged at his brain. Was there something, anything, he could have done to sabotage this whole operation?

What could he possibly have done when the only thing he had any control over was the drug itself?

Was that it? Had he somehow tampered with the drug?

"Quesada, get me the reports on the test subjects we

gave the new drug to, now!" he shouted. Panic began to form in his gut as fear that this whole operation could come crumbling down around him filled him with a tingling apprehension.

"As you wish, Patron," Quesada answered.

He watched as the big man got on his phone to call the test area and the people watching over the subjects, or rather, addicts, to whom they had given a sample of the drug to test its viability. He saw the expression change from confusion at the sudden request to worry as he received bad news.

"What, what is it?" he shouted across at his friend.

"Patron, they are all dead," Quesada said in shock.

"How? When?" Moya wanted to know.

"They say they all died within twenty-four hours of having been administered the new drug. At first, they thought it was because they were all addicts, that it was an overdose. But they did further tests, and they found out that it was the drug that killed them. Again, they thought it was the dosage and that they had given them a too-pure form of it, but after further testing, it revealed it was the drug. No matter what the dosage was, it was lethal. Patron, if that drug is released, you will be the biggest mass murderer in the history of this country, maybe even the world," Quesada said.

A shout erupted from somewhere in the room, and it was seconds before Moya realized it was him shouting. His anger and frustration at being thwarted this close to the finish line was devastating. He sank to his knees, holding his head in his hands.

He stood up, his legs trembling with the effort, and he held out a hand to steady himself against a nearby desk.

Looking around at the faces of everyone present, he saw the shock in their eyes.

Finding his voice, he shouted, "Find Franklin and kill him."

CHAPTER THIRTY

Car sirens blasted through the still of the night as vehicles approached emblazoned with the letters DEA on the hoods and sides.

"Here's that diversion you wanted," Jack said.

"I was hoping to stay outta prison a little while longer though," Charley told him when she saw the vehicles come to a screeching halt at the front gates.

"We can sneak in while they're causing all this commotion at the front," Jack said, walking off toward one of the other gates.

There was an employee entrance a short walk from where they had watched the DEA arrive, and it was guarded by only one man.

"Show your badge, your ID, or whatever you guys carry, and we should be able to bluff our way in," Jack said.

They walked confidently to the gate. The guard, whose attention up to that point was on all the fuss at the front, turned to greet them.

Before he could say anything, Charley took out her

ID and flashed it to him, saying, "I'm with them, and he's with me. We have reason to believe there's someone of interest inside here. More than that, I can't tell you, I'm sorry. Ya know how it is, buddy?"

"Preachin' to the converted ma'am," he replied and opened the gates a little wider for them to enter.

"Now we're in, let's do this," she said.

———

Moya heard all the sirens and turned to Quesada, a questioning expression on his dark features.

Before he could ask the question, Quesada said, "I'll go see what it is, Patron."

Moya watched as he left the room, his phone already to his ear as he made the call.

Sirens could only mean one thing, cops.

What the hell were they doing here, and why now? He thought he had enough of them in his pocket so they wouldn't ever bother him. He even had a top-level agent in the DEA to keep him informed should any investigation lead them to him. What went wrong? Was this a power play for more money, or was it something else?

Quesada came back, and the shock in his eyes was evident.

"It is the DEA, Patron."

"What the fuck are they doing here?" Moya shouted in fury. "Why weren't we informed they were coming?"

"They say they had a tip-off that a rogue agent was last seen entering the area," Quesada told him.

Moya took a step away as he processed what he'd been told.

A rogue DEA agent seen here? Why? He thought.

"It can only be the agent who helped Franklin escape.

She's come here to try and stop the delivery," he said as it all became clear to him.

"If that is true, Patron, then she won't be alone. She had help, and you can bet whoever it was will be here with her now," Quesada reasoned.

"Get the men to patrol the area, find her, and we can deliver her body to the DEA to get them out of here," Moya instructed.

"What about the DEA, Patron? What should we do about them?"

"Delay them as long as you can, if you can't, then steer them away from the containers where the drones are stored. Nothing will delay the delivery."

Quesada looked at him through narrowed eyes, not sure if he'd heard him correctly.

"You are going ahead with it then?" he asked, not sure what to expect.

"Why not? Why waste all that money on the drugs and not use them?" Moya countered.

"Because it will kill thousands, maybe millions of people, Patron. Do you want to do that? I mean, *really* do that? I have been your friend for many years, and I trust you with my life, so whatever you choose, I will be by your side all the way, but if you go down this road, you have to know what will happen to you, to us. The rest of the world will hunt us down for the rest of our lives. There will be nowhere on Earth where we will be safe."

Moya looked at him. What he said had merit, there was absolute truth in his words, but he had a path to follow, a destiny. He was destined to be the ruler of a great dynasty in the drug world. He was going to unite all the cartels under his name. It was all there though, his destiny was still clear, and somehow Franklin, in his own path of revenge, had handed him the perfect opportunity with this new drug of his. He would still unite the cartels because once the drug was released, it would wipe out all the addicts in the world and all his competitors too. Then it was just a matter of starting afresh, and if the cartels wanted any part of his new enterprise, they would have to pledge fealty to him.

"Why not? We can still win this. This can still work in our favor. We distribute the drug, we wipe out the other cartels by destroying their customer base, then we start all over again, and the cartels will have to join us to survive. With all that power behind us, they can come for us, but no one will dare stop us. We'll be unstoppable. Xavier, we'll be Gods," Moya said, his eyes glinting with the fervor he now felt for his chosen path.

He saw Quesada look at him. Moya knew his friend had seen him in all his various moods. He'd been at his side when the attack on his villa killed his wife and son, but the look in his friend's eyes when he looked at him at that moment was something new. He had never seen him look at him like this before, it was something completely new. It was more like fear.

"Are you with me, Xavier?" he asked.

"Yes, Patron, always."

"Then go, do what you have to. Time is running out."

CHAPTER THIRTY-ONE

The dock area was covered with large metal containers stacked three high with just enough space on the ground between each row for walking space.

There was an office set apart from them where all the admin was done.

Jack and Charley saw this as they approached as quietly as they could. Jack needed to know where this shipment of drones was being stored, and he still had no idea how he was going to stop them as yet. Finding them was his first priority, the rest would come when he had their location.

"Have you any idea where they will be?" he asked Charley as she stood by his side at the edge of a row of tall containers.

"Didn't Franklin say that we'd know when it was time or something like that?" she pointed out.

"What did he mean by that, I wonder?" Jack mused as he looked around at the containers. All the containers were stacked with doors on the side so they could be loaded from the front when on the ground.

Something suddenly occurred to him.

"How does Moya plan on releasing the drones?" he asked, turning back to look at Charley, his eyes on fire with the revelation that had just hit him.

He saw her come to the same realization he just had.

"The containers have to be on top somewhere so he can release them through the top straight into the sky," she replied with a smile crossing her lovely face.

Another thought hit Jack then.

"That just made destroying them a whole lot harder," he said.

"I know! How the fuck do we get up to them, get inside, and destroy them without causing millions of dollars of destruction to everything else stored here?" confirming his thoughts.

———

Moya made his way to the office where the person controlling the release of the drones had taken over. It was his job to input the code to begin the countdown and then monitor the automatic opening of the top doors of the specially constructed containers holding the drones that would then activate the drones inside. Basically, he just had to be there in case anything went wrong, but if it worked as planned, there was nothing that could be done to stop them from continuing on their pre-set program.

The drones would continue to their destination and carry out the rest of their programming, which was the release of the drug over the populated areas of Miami.

The residents would not know what was happening, but all the addicts soon would. They would exhibit signs of the effect of the drug within hours, according to the new reports he had from the doctors watching over the test subjects. Within hours all the addicts in Miami would begin to die, and after a few days, the city would be free of this plague. He would have no customers, but that was just a slight setback, nothing more than a glitch in his destiny. He would soon have a new set of customers clambering for his new, improved product, and he would be in charge of the drug trade in the entire country and, pretty soon after that, the entire world.

"Is everything ready?" he asked as he entered the office.

"Everything is in place, Patron, the program is ready. I just have to input the code for the program to begin, and then everything will continue as planned," he said with reverence.

"Go ahead and input the code then," Moya told him. He watched as he turned to the console and input the ten-digit code that would start the program.

Once that was done, he turned to Moya. "It is done, Patron," he said.

"Good, you have done great work, Hector. I will ensure you and your family are well looked after, you have my word," Moya said.

He checked the time against his Tag Heuer Aquaracer watch to make sure the countdown was correct. They now had ten minutes before the drones were released from the containers, and his destiny would be fulfilled.

———

A creaking sound of tortured metal alerted both Jack and Charley. Both of them looked up to where the sound was coming from.

The top of the container they were standing below started to open up. The top split into two down the middle, with each side opening up on huge hinges attached from the side. Jack saw the nearest door flip slowly upright and then stop.

"He's releasing the drones," Jack said.

"We're too late," Charley added.

"Not if I have anything to say about it," Jack said. He looked around for something.

Charley asked, "What're you looking for?"

"They have to be controlling this from somewhere. It has to be close. The range on those drones isn't infinite, so to set them off, they have to be within range. We need to find the office," he quickly explained.

With a new determination in her eyes, Charley said, "This way, c'mon."

As they rounded the corner of the nearest container, a voice boomed out across the open dock area.

"Freeze!"

"Shit!" Jack exclaimed as he dragged Charley back out of view.

Bullets zinged off the side of the container as the DEA agents opened fire on them.

"C'mon, back this way," Jack instructed towards the other end of the container alley.

As the two of them ran back into the maze of alleys between all the containers, bullets chased them, ricocheting off the walls, zinging around the alley they were in, causing more danger.

Jack turned right at the end, and Charley followed close on his heels.

Adrenaline was flooding his system as all his senses went on high alert. He had to control the fight or flight reflex that came with this response and respond calmly. If he allowed panic to take over, he would get them both killed. He was too good a soldier to allow that to happen though.

At the end of the container, he stopped and pressed his back to it, peering around to see how many people were after them.

"Since when did the DEA take on a shoot-on-sight policy?" he asked as Charley joined him.

"It seems my suspicions about Harper were correct. He can't allow me to tell the truth of what happened at the safe house, or his career is finished," she said, breathing hard.

"It's a pity we can't shoot back at them."

"Fuck that! Anyone who has the balls to shoot at me will soon learn the error of their ways," Charley snarled angrily.

Both of them took out their weapons and jacked the slides, injecting rounds into the chambers.

More bullets pinged off the side of the container as the DEA agents opened fire once more. Ducking, Jack moved out of the way of more gunfire. He fired a rapid three-shot salvo around the corner to put off any more gunfire, then turned.

He ran towards the opposite end of the container, followed by Charley again. Time was running out for them faster than he wanted. The drones would be released very soon, and they were still no closer to finding a way of stopping the release of the drug.

"This is getting us nowhere fast," Charley said.

Jack had to agree, he heard the sound of heavy footsteps running towards them from the front of the dock area.

He stopped at the corner of one of the containers just in time to see two DEA agents run into view.

Jack moved fast. He struck the nearest agent in the

face with the butt of his Walther, knocking him back into the other agent. He kicked the agent's knee sideways, dislocating the joint.

The agent collapsed in an agonizing heap.

A right cross to the side of the jaw put his lights out, and it was game over.

The other agent regained his composure, and Jack saw the shock in his eyes as his partner went down. It had just occurred to him that he may have bitten off more than he could chew.

He tried to bring up his pistol to fire. Jack saw the movement in time and blocked the arm. His right hand came across, blocking the weapon as he stepped into close quarters with the agent. In one swift-flowing movement, he brought his right elbow back, smashing the point into the face of the agent. His head was sent back in a shower of blood as his nose was splashed across his face. Turning to face the agent, Jack punched him square in the jaw. The blow knocked his head back as his eyes rolled up inside his skull. He fell over flat on his back, unconscious.

The two agents had been taken out in less than thirty seconds.

"You certainly don't take prisoners," Charley said, her eyes wide in appreciation of his skills.

"Let's go," he said, avoiding making any comment.

There was open ground in front of them as the dock area faced them. Berthed at the edge were several cargo ships. The water stretched out for miles as the bay opened out in front of them.

The office was not in sight. It would be far from the front of the water so that the heavy movers could load the cargo containers onto the waiting ships. It would be situated at the rear of the loading area, nestled in some corner, away from where all the work was done but with a clear view of the front.

By the time Jack realized they had completely gone in the wrong direction, it was almost too late.

He grabbed Charley's hand and ducked down into the space between two large containers dragging her with him.

More bullets followed them as they ran. Ricochets pinged off the sides of the metal containers coming so close Jack felt one crease his clothes and another the skin on his face.

"They certainly don't want us to succeed," Jack said.

"Fuck this," Charley said, turning back, her gun drawn and ready to fire. The first DEA agent she saw coming around the side of a container she shot. The agent dropped like a stone.

"Maybe they'll think twice about fucking with us now," she uttered angrily.

"We're running out of time," Jack said.

They came to an opening and sprinted for the next gap between the containers. As he reached it, bullets pinged off the side of the metal.

Jack grabbed Charley and dragged her with him to prevent her from killing any more of the DEA agents. Speed was their only option now. They had to find the office and fast, before the drones started their delivery run.

In the distance, he saw a small building with an upstairs section that was brightly lit from inside. The large windows that ran around the exterior showed activity inside.

"That's it," he said.

There was a staircase that ran up the outside of the

building to a door at the top, which seemed like the only way in or out.

Jack peered around the side of the container before moving out. There was no one in sight, so he sprinted across the open space and reached the bottom of the staircase in a few moments. Charley followed on his heels, and as he grabbed onto the railing of the staircase to pull himself up, he heard her right behind him.

They ran up the stairs and Jack threw open the door. Inside were two men standing over by a desk. It was the control center of the docks. Everything could be overseen here, and one man was working while the other was simply watching.

Jack knew this second man even though he'd never seen him before.

"Give it up, Moya, it's over," he said, aiming his Walther at him.

Before anything could be said or done, gunfire from below the stairs ripped apart the doorframe.

The two operatives dashed inside to avoid getting shot.

From over by the desk, Jack heard Moya say, "You are too late, it's done."

Jack turned to see what he meant as Moya aimed a pistol at the man with him. He shot him in the head, sending him to the floor, then turned his gun on the console, firing several bullets into it until sparks flew and smoke started to billow out from the interior workings. Flames erupted on the desk as the equipment was destroyed.

"We need to get out of here," Jack told Charley.

Moya disappeared through a door on the opposite side of the room, another staircase that had been invisible from their vantage point on the outside as they approached, and he was gone.

The two of them dashed across the room, hoping to escape the shooters and catch Moya. He was their only hope of preventing the drugs from being distributed, but as the fire grew in the room, Jack doubted they would be able to do that now.

As they ran down the stairs, the room above exploded in a fireball that spread, soon engulfing the entire top floor of the building.

Flaming debris rained down on them, and they quickly ran between the nearest containers.

"What now?" Charley asked, looking up at the fire and then at Jack.

He had nothing, and as he looked up at the other containers, he saw the drones start to fly. The sky was soon filled with the small craft as their rotors spun, lifting them into the air and then off on their pre-programmed route toward the mainland.

Before he could say anything, the two of them were surrounded by armed DEA agents, all aiming their weapons at them.

"Freeze, place your hands on your heads slowly, and get on your knees," one of them ordered.

Jack looked at her as he complied and said, "It's over, we lost."

CHAPTER THIRTY-TWO

As the two operatives kneeled down, their hands were handcuffed behind them, then they were dragged to their feet. Jack noticed they all remained quiet as they deferred to someone else, probably the agent in charge. He didn't have to wait long to see who it was.

"Bill Harper, I didn't think you'd have the balls to show up in person," Charley spat her accusation at him.

"Put the two of them in my car," Harper said to one of the agents, then, as a precaution, added, "and be careful, these two are tricky."

"The drones have been released, Bill. Thousands are about to die. Doesn't that mean anything to you, or would you prefer to just take your bribe and turn a blind eye to it all?" Charley shouted as they were taken away.

Jack saw one of the agents look at Harper and ask, "What the hell is she talking about, Bill?"

"Nothing, she's trying to deflect, that's all. Take no notice of anything she says," he replied.

"But the drones are flying, and they seem to be

heading for the city, so what does she mean thousands will die? What's on those drones, Bill?" the agent asked.

Jack saw his opportunity then, "Felix Moya has had a drug engineered to overpower any addict's cravings and turn them onto his drug. What he didn't know was that the chemist made it so it was fatal to any addict. He's just released a deadly drug that's going to be dispersed over Miami. By morning every addict in the city will be dead," he shouted.

The agent halted the others taking Jack and Charley away. He looked at Jack, trying to figure out what was really going on here.

"Why would a drug lord kill off all his clients?" he asked. "It doesn't make sense."

"He didn't know. He thought the drug would simply make them addicted to his drug, thereby cutting out the competition and ensuring the market was his alone. The chemist he used had an axe to grind. To force him to work for him, Moya kidnapped the chemist's daughter and made her an addict too. They told him if he did as they wanted, they would get her clean. Instead, they killed her as she had a low tolerance to the drugs they filled her with, so he plotted his revenge. Making the drug lethal was his way of getting back both at Moya and the addicts he despised," Jack explained quickly. He knew he had one chance of getting this agent on their side. If Harper persuaded them to put them in his car, they would surely be killed if he was indeed working for the cartel, as Charley suspected.

The agent said, "This is all very nice, but can you prove any of it?"

"No, but all you have to do is wait twelve hours, and then you'll start to see the effects for yourself," Jack said coldly.

He saw the agent mull this over, and he had to push his point home.

"Ask Harper there, he knows. He's been working for Moya this whole time. He ran an operation to get an agent inside the cartel. He actually turned one of Moya's men, got him to talk to Franklin, the chemist, and that man's contact was Charley, agent Parker here. The only contact she had was with Harper. He knew what was going on all the time, but when he found out about what Franklin had done, he tried to shut Agent Parker down from informing anyone at the DEA. Harper has been working both sides this whole time," he said.

The agent turned to Harper then and said, "Is any of this true, Bill?"

Harper looked away with derision and said, "Tony, you know me...would I take a bribe?"

"I don't know, Bill, would you?"

Harper reached for his service pistol, "Oh fuck this," he said, then shot Tony and the other two agents around them. He turned to the two agents holding Jack and Charley and fired another shot, dropping one of them. To the last one, he said, "Take them to my car, now."

Jack speared Harper with a look of pure venom. "You can't get away with killing all these agents, you have to know that, Bill," he said calmly.

"You're joking, right? I turn out to be the hero of this story. I caught you two. You managed to shoot and kill the agents with me but died in a shoot-out as you tried to escape. Simple when you know how."

"Sounds like you've done this before," Jack commented.

"Oh, you're not the first person I've had to silence who cottoned on to my little side job, but now here's the thing, I always get away with it," Harper replied smugly.

Charley indicated the agent with them, "What about him?"

Harper glanced at him, saw the worried look on his face, then shot him in the face.

"Yeah, you're right, you killed him too."

It was just the three of them left, and Jack knew he had to do something fast, or they'd both end up face-down in the dirt with the other agents.

"How do you explain ballistics? They'll learn all the bullets came from one gun, yours," Jack said.

"Simple again, you managed to get my gun away from me, but I wrestled it from you and shot the two of you as a last resort, but not before you killed everyone with me," he said, smiling.

"So, are you gonna kill us here?" Charley asked. Jack knew she was stalling for time.

"Oh no, you're coming with me. Once I've gotten away, I'll dispose of you, then radio in to tell the DEA what happened. You see, you took me prisoner, but I managed to get away, get my gun back from you, and kill you both as retribution for killing all my agent friends. God, I'm heroic," he said, laughing.

"Well, you seem to have thought of everything, Bill. I have to give it to you, you certainly can think on your feet," Jack said, hoping to disarm him, to make him think they'd given up.

"Yeah, yeah, I'm not falling for that. Get moving, we've a long drive ahead of us," he said, indicating the direction he wanted them to go with a wave of the gun.

"Where are we going?" Charley asked.

"You'll see when we get there," was all Harper would say.

Jack gave Charley a glance that said, 'we're not finished yet', and he moved off.

Where was he taking them? He had a little time to try and free his hands, once he'd done that, he could overpower Harper when he saw his opportunity, but at the moment, he would just have to go along with it. There was nothing he could do except wait for the right time to act.

As they reached the SUV, Harper's phone went off. Taking it from his pocket, he held it to his ear.

"Get in the back," he told Jack and Charley, who complied by climbing into the back seats. Jack saw Harper close the door and step away as he held his pistol trained on them while he took the call.

From his expression, he was taking orders which he wasn't too keen on. He put the phone away after a brief discussion and then got behind the wheel.

Jack said, "Here we go."

CHAPTER THIRTY-THREE

SECTION ZERO HQ, LONDON

Tony Armstrong strode into Bennett's office with a worried look on his face.

"What's wrong?" Bennett asked.

"We just received word that the DEA lost several of their agents, and they're blaming it on a rogue DEA agent and a British operative who were working together with the Moya Cartel."

Bennett looked up at him, "Harper is bending the truth just as Parker said he would."

"I thought you were going to see that the DEA would stay off their backs," Tony accused.

"Harper is driving the narrative now. There is only so much weight I carry with the DEA, and apparently, his word carries more."

"So, are you saying there's nothing we can do to help them?" Tony asked.

Bennett shook his head. "Do you have faith in your man, Colonel?"

"What's that supposed to mean?" Tony asked, stepping forward.

"I'll overlook the adversarial attitude for now, Colonel, as you are worried about your man, I get that. You didn't answer my question though. Do you have faith in your man?" Bennett said calmly.

"Jack is possibly the best man we've ever had working for us. That's why Bainbridge gave him so much slack when he wanted time off to be with his family. We thought it best to allow it rather than lose him completely. He is the best at what he does," Tony said finally.

"Then you have to trust that he'll get the job done. I will do what I can, but ultimately, while he's out in the field, he is on his own."

Tony nodded, "You're right, but that doesn't make me like it any more, sir."

"I understand, Tony. What works for me is I concentrate on the things I actually have a chance of controlling. The rest, I try not to concern myself with too much. It's wasted energy to worry about anything you have no control over."

As Tony was about to leave, Bennett asked, "Have you still got Jack's location, are you able to track his phone's GPS?"

"Yes, sir, he's still in Miami."

"Keep an eye on him. When he's ready or able, no doubt he'll call for backup, and it's our job to get it to him as fast as we can."

"Who have we got available?"

"I've already had words with some contacts in the US DEA through diplomatic channels, and they said they would help however they could. I'm sorry, Colonel, but at the moment, that's all I can do."

Tony smiled. This wasn't the news he was hoping for. Nodding, he said, "I'll keep you updated, sir," before leaving the office.

Once Armstrong had left and Bennett was alone once more, he thought about what Franklin had told him. Moya sounded insane, but things were firmly in the hands of Jack Cross and Charley Parker. He hoped they could hold on.

―――――

Moya was driving away from Port Miami with Quesada sitting beside him.

Moya had escaped from the office after leaving it in disarray, then ran to his vehicle, where he called Quesada to meet him. His minder had been busy redirecting DEA agents toward the two other agents Harper had allowed to escape. Moya's anger had been like a raging fire when he saw them invade the office, and had it not been for his quick reaction, things could have turned out very differently.

As he had waited for Quesada to arrive, he had called Harper, who he had seen capture the two insufferable intruders.

"Where to Patron?" Quesada asked as he took the wheel of the SUV.

"Back to the chopper. By the time we get home, we will have some guests, and the rest of my plan can be put into play."

Quesada was curious as he drove the SUV out of the parking lot and away from the port. Moya could tell he wanted to ask him something. He saved him the trouble by speaking first, "I suppose you're wondering what my intentions are, my friend?"

His minder simply looked at him and gave a brief nod.

"The authorities will soon know what I am capable of. They will be desperate not to see the same thing happen in every city across the country, so they will pay me millions to prevent it from happening."

"Do you think the other cartels will allow you to control the entire trade though, my Patron?" Quesada asked, unconvinced.

"They will have little choice. They either bow to my control, or I wipe them out. There is enough to go around. I can combine all the cartels under one master. Together we will rule the world. We will have enough power to topple governments or make them bow to our will. My friend, our destiny is within our grasp, finally. Just a little longer, and we will be the most powerful men on the planet," Moya said with complete honesty.

He saw his friend and confidant of the past few years look at him and saw the doubt in his eyes.

He would see, as they all would see, his destiny was to rule, and that destiny was about to come true.

Jack and Charley sat in the rear of the SUV as Harper drove them away from PortMiami.

The two of them were in the rear, still with their hands bound and restrained so that Harper could drive the vehicle without any fear of their escape.

Charley leaned in to whisper in Jack's ear, "I think he's taking us to the airport."

"Any ideas where he could be taking us?" Jack asked. He had a few of his own, but he wanted her input as he felt she had a better handle on the situation than him.

He'd come into this pretty much blind and was busy playing catch up more or less the whole time.

"A couple," she said, "and you won't like either of them."

Jack nodded, knowing she was right because his theories weren't much better either.

"What're we going to do then?" he asked to see if she had a plan.

"Not much we can do yet. I guess we just wait and see where we end up."

"And what if we end up somewhere surrounded by armed men?" he asked, putting the worst-case scenario out there.

"We'll just have to figure that out when the time arrives, I suppose."

Reluctantly Jack had to agree for the time being.

The two of them sat back and waited. The journey continued in silence as Harper drove them to the airport.

Harper drove the SUV to the private section where a DEA chopper was waiting with the rotors already turning as the engine was being spooled up.

"Out!" Harper ordered the two passengers under gunpoint.

"Do I have to ask?" Jack said.

"You're a bright boy, where do you think?" Harper asked.

Jack and Charley walked over to the chopper and climbed aboard. Harper followed and then gave the signal for the pilot to lift off.

Harper sat opposite them with a headset on his head so he could talk to the pilot. He looked at the two of them and moved the mic down from in front of his mouth to speak to them. "Don't worry, this will all be over soon."

Now that his mic was back up and the fact they hadn't got headsets of their own, Jack and Charley couldn't be heard, and by the look in Harper's eye, he didn't care.

Jack had a feeling about where they were being taken, and his stomach lurched at the prospect.

CHAPTER THIRTY-FOUR

SECTION ZERO HQ, LONDON

Bennett picked up the phone at his elbow. He knew who was calling by the number that was flashing on the cradle.

"Tony, what have you got for me?"

"I don't know if you want to hear this, sir. We're still tracking Jack's phone, and he's on board a chopper heading for Columbia. We picked up some chatter about the incident at PortMiami, and there was talk about an agent ferrying two prisoners to the airport."

"So, this confirms what Agent Parker said about Agent Harper being on Moya's payroll. I can't imagine any other reason why he would take them into Columbia."

"You're right, sir. I'm not sure what we can do though," Tony said.

"Section Zero is supposed to be just that, Colonel, zero, naught, nothing. We don't exist, so at the moment, there is nothing we can do. As a member of the Security Services, I could ask a favor of the DEA, but that's all I can do. Jack and Agent Parker are on their own, I'm afraid."

"I thought you'd say that, sir."

"I am hearing something in your voice, Colonel, that I am not sure I want to. I hope you're not thinking of doing something foolish?"

"Plausible deniability, sir, just remember that," Tony said and hung up.

Despite what Tony had said, Bennett knew he was going to do something. He wondered how Bainbridge had coped all those years with operatives like this going off book all the time.

―――

"We're not going to Washington DC, where the DEA HQ is," Charley said to Jack raising her voice to be heard over the engine noise in the chopper.

Jack looked at Harper, who was watching them with complete disdain. He could tell by how he dismissed their conversation that he considered there was nothing they could do to prevent the inevitable.

Jack turned to Charley and said, "No prizes for knowing where he's taking us then."

Charley shook her head.

Jack saw Harper stifle a smile which told him the DEA agent could either read lips or he deduced what they had realized.

His hands were cuffed behind his back still, but in his hand, secreted away from the prying eyes of the DEA agents who captured them, he held a paperclip. He had seen an opportunity to grab one off the nearest desk when they invaded the office back at Port Miami to stop

Moya. He knew capture by the agents was inevitable, so he took steps, just in case.

Now as he sat in the chopper, he maneuvered the clip into both hands where he had straightened it out. The difficulty was not being able to see what he was doing and not to give any signs away of what he was doing to the agent in front of them, who, no matter how indifferent he tried to appear, Jack knew he was watching them like a hawk.

He inserted the tip of the clip into the lock of his handcuffs, and after a few seconds of twisting and maneuvering it into place, he felt a satisfying 'click' as the lock opened. He did the same with the other cuff and was soon free of them. He kept his hands behind him as he didn't want to alert Harper to the change in their circumstances.

If they were going to where he suspected, then maybe there was a chance of ending all this, once and for all.

Jack hatched an escape plan and revenge for all the lives that were going to be lost in the next few hours, but it had one flaw. If the one deciding factor was not in place, then they were heading into the lion's den with no way of getting out alive and no way of preventing further deaths.

———

COLOMBIA

Moya walked into his villa, followed by Quesada. The chopper they had arrived in was parked on the back lawn where a helipad was situated.

"They'll be here soon, Patron," Quesada said as he followed Moya.

"Get the men ready. I'm going to prepare, I have a world to contact," Moya told him in all seriousness. The two of them separated, with Quesada going to where the men were berthed as Moya went into the villa.

The repairs were well underway by this time. The wall had been rebuilt, and the interior was looking cleaner, with some of the furniture back in place.

He went through the main lounge into his office at the back of the villa, where he had a computer. Sitting down at his desk, he booted up the computer. He connected to the internet and sat back, thinking about the best way to go about what he was going to do.

To maximize the effect of what he was going to say, he chose to post the video live on one of the social media outlets that were free to use. That way, the Americans couldn't hide it from the public. The more panic he caused around the globe, the more certain he was to get what he wanted.

He activated the camera and accessed the channel he wanted, then began to speak.

"My name is Felix Moya, I am a drug lord, and you are going to want to hear what I have to say because it will change all your lives."

CHAPTER THIRTY-FIVE

Jack looked out the window of the chopper, hoping for some sign as to where they were headed.

The ground below was filled with rolling hills cut through with dirt tracks that pretended to be roads. Obviously, the only way that anyone could navigate through the area was by vehicle.

In the distance, he saw a building that he immediately recognized as the Moya villa. It was showing signs of repair from the recent attack by his rival cartel.

Harper was looking at him and must have seen the recognition in his eyes as he leaned forward to speak to him.

"Yes, we're almost there. I told you this would soon be over," he said, sitting back with a smile.

Jack said as loudly as he could, "It sort of throws your plans to lay the blame for those agents' deaths on us out the window though, if we turn up dead here. Doesn't it? I mean, how're you going to explain that little fact to the DEA back home?"

Harper's smile faded for a second. Then he went to

lean forward once more to taunt Jack again. Jack mirrored his movement, but as the agent held his pistol loosely in front of him, confident he was in control, Jack struck.

He brought his arms around to the front and hit Harper in the throat with a straight fingers jab.

The agent's eyes went wide with the shock, and he almost let go of the weapon. Jack grabbed the hand holding the pistol, brought it up under Harper's chin, and fired twice. The two bullets went through Harper's skull in an explosion of blood and brain matter, painting the top of the cabin in gore.

Jack was out of his seat in a flash, heading forward to the cabin where the pilot sat. He saw his head turn to see what was going on. The sight of him coming at him galvanized him into action. He turned the cyclic control over to the left, turning the chopper into a tight turn. The momentum threw Jack in that direction, and he slammed into the seat next to the pilot. The force took him into the seat and past it, and before he could correct his movement, he found himself flat against the door. The gun he held in his hand had dropped the instant he slammed into the door, and he didn't have the time to root around for it.

Jack pushed himself back into the cabin, turning to face the pilot who had reached for a pistol.

With his left hand, Jack blocked the pistol as it fired. The bullet narrowly missed his head as it passed by, going through the front window. The sound of the gunshot so close sent a shockwave through his head, almost perforating his eardrums. The pain was sudden and intense, but he knew he couldn't let it incapacitate him.

He slammed his right fist against the side of the pilot's jaw to persuade him not to use the gun again.

Holding the pistol in his left hand, he chopped the wrist with his right hand. The pilot's fingers went numb from the blow, and he released his grip on the pistol.

Flying a chopper one-handed was never a good thing; you needed both hands on the controls, so the instant the pilot reached for the pistol, the chopper's attitude had altered. The machine was now flying erratically, which threw Jack around in the cabin as he wrestled with the pilot for control.

With one hand on the control and the other being held by his attacker, the pilot was unable to defend himself adequately against Jack's repeated punches to his face.

Jack saw the man go limp after his last punch, so he slammed a hand against the harness release button. The straps came loose, and he reached across to open the door, then pushed him out into the air.

The chopper immediately went into a spin with no one at the controls, and Jack thought he'd killed them both for a second as he quickly scrambled into the vacated seat. Grabbing both the cyclic and collective controls, then placing his feet on the anti-torque pedals, he pulled back on the controls to bring the aircraft around on an even keel.

"Are you alright back there?" he asked when he was sure the chopper was under his control.

Charley came through from the back to sit next to him. "I am now," she said with a huge grin.

Jack had passed the paper clip he had used to unlock his handcuffs to her without Harper knowing just before he made his move.

"I almost dropped that clip you passed me twice while you were fighting with the pilot," she told him, still grinning.

"You look like you're having fun."

"I'm just glad we got free, man, I also wished it had been me who shot that bastard Harper, but hey, you roll with what you got."

Jack concentrated on flying the chopper then and getting his bearings.

"Do you think they saw you throw the pilot out?" Charley asked as she strapped herself in.

"We're about to find out."

When she saw where they were heading, she asked, "Wait, are you still thinking of taking us in?"

Jack didn't look at her because he knew there was no good way of telling her his plan without it sounding crazy.

"Jack, what the fuck is going on here, man?"

"Okay, listen," Jack started. Both of them were wearing the headsets now, so they didn't have to shout to be heard anymore. "I have a theory, and I know you won't like it, that's why I hesitated in telling you."

"Go on, I'm listening," uncertain, she wanted to hear what he was about to say.

"I doubt Franklin would have made this drug without some sort of safeguard in case people he loved were infected, like his daughter. He wouldn't have wanted her to be killed along with all the others," Jack said.

"So, your theory relies on the good doc making an antidote for his killer drug, is that it?"

"Pretty much, yes," Jack agreed. He saw she wasn't convinced by how her eyes went wide, and she looked away. "I'm thinking he put his plan in motion as soon as they forced him to do their bidding. After all, they did say they would get his daughter clean and let the two of them go once he had finished. I'm thinking he made the drug a killer to get back at them but had a contingency plan in case they went back on their word, you know, to protect both him and her."

"It's a pretty big assumption."

"I know, but it's all we have. If he didn't have a plan like this, then there is no way we can stop Moya from spreading his drug anywhere he wants. We already failed to prevent him from infecting Miami. I won't fail anyone else," Jack said, his face set in determination.

"Any ideas on how we're getting inside?"

"How about we knock on the front door?"

CHAPTER THIRTY-SIX

SECTION ZERO HQ

Bennett was sitting at his desk staring at the monitor screen when his phone rang.

Picking up the handset, he listened. He already knew who was calling and, after seeing the video, had expected it.

"I assume you're watching this?" the Prime Minister said.

"Yes, sir, I am."

"Well, our American cousins are not sweeping this under the rug now, are they?" the PM said.

"I very much doubt that, sir."

"This is a total mess, one which I'm sure the Americans will be eager to forget ever happened. Are you and your section looking into this matter?"

"I have my man looking into it as we speak, sir," Bennett said guardedly.

Chambers recognized what he was doing and said, "Okay, I see. In that case, I'll let you get on with it. Let me know when you have a result we can use," and then he hung up.

As Bennett sat there, he thought about Jack Cross and agent Charley Parker, sent into the lion's den with no backup. He had sent agents into dire situations before, not personally though. As Deputy Director, he gave the order, but it was someone else who issued it to the agents in question. This was the first time he had ever come this close to that sort of decision-making, and he wasn't sure if he could do it again. He had made contact with Cross, he came close to knowing him, so this had an effect that he hadn't accounted for.

He just hoped those two had what it took to get the job done, if not, then millions of people would die.

———

COLOMBIA

"Maybe we don't have to knock on the front door," Charley said. This caught Jack's attention.

"How do you mean?"

"Franklin would have a lab somewhere close so that Moya could keep an eye on him, but it wouldn't be in the villa."

Jack knew what they had to do then. "He had a lab somewhere else. Of course he did. Moya wouldn't allow drugs to be made anywhere close to his family, but it would be close enough for his guard dogs to keep an eye on the operation. Is there an annex or somewhere like that anywhere nearby?" he asked.

"Exactly like that. Franklin called it the annex, it is just south of here. That's where we need to go," she said.

Jack turned the chopper in that direction and headed towards the annex.

"Is there anywhere we can land this thing without them seeing us?" Jack asked.

"He told me once that usually there was only one guard stationed on ground level. The lab he worked in was underground, so we need to get down there."

Jack saw it then, a Helipad set at the rear of the building on a well-manicured lawn. He adjusted the controls to take the aircraft down to land behind the building.

"Right, let's go," he said to Charley as he unbuckled his harness.

The two of them approached from the rear of the building and stopped at the side. Standing in front of the entrance was a guard. He was wearing an earpiece which meant he was connected to other guards, probably down in the lab and possibly the main villa too. They would have to eliminate him without alerting the others.

Before Jack could say anything, Charley said, "I have an idea, get ready to move."

Jack was about to ask what she had in mind, but she was off, heading across the back of the building towards the opposite side.

Suspecting he knew what she was about to do, he watched her disappear around the corner, then went back to peer around the front and got ready for her to make her move.

The guard's attention was immediately drawn to her as she appeared at his right side, and Jack made his move. As she engaged him, he made his way across the front of the building, approaching the guard from behind as silently as he could.

"Don't move a muscle, or I will shoot you where you

stand," Jack said as he pressed the muzzle of his gun into the back of the guard's head.

Charley tilted her head in an apology to him and said, "Sorry, maybe another time? No, you're right, you're not my type anyway."

She relieved him of his assault rifle and searched inside his jacket for his sidearm.

Jack came around the front keeping his pistol aimed at the man's face.

"How do we get down there?" he asked. "Before you even think of alerting them down there, don't. I will kill you, make no mistake about that. Tell me what I want to know, and I'll let you live, do anything rash, and you die. It's as simple as that. It's your choice, choose wisely," he added, staring into his eyes and gauging his reaction. This was a low-level thug who didn't particularly want to die, but Moya had instilled in all his employees a fear of him that transcended any other. Jack saw the change in his attitude and knew what was coming.

With a nod, the thug said, "Go to hell."

Jack fired his weapon painting the guard's brains across the front of the building.

"So, how do we get inside then?" Charley asked, looking from the corpse on the ground up to Jack.

Before he could reply, she said, "And don't say, knock on the door."

Declining to answer, Jack instead turned his attention toward the door. At the side of this was a panel with a small screen on it.

"This is a retina scanner," he said, then began to pick up the dead guard and stood him up. Charley helped him, trying not to get the man's blood all over her, and the two of them took him to the scanner. Jack held one of his eyes open and placed his face close to the scanner, hoping that the close proximity was all that was needed to activate it.

Sure enough, the door opened to reveal an elevator.

Releasing the dead guard, the two of them entered the elevator. Charley pulled back on the lever on the assault rifle, injecting a round into the breach, while Jack checked his own pistol as the elevator doors closed and started its descent to the lower levels.

Jack looked at Charley, "Are you ready for this?"

She nodded her assent and stared ahead. He could see her focus was entirely on the job ahead of them. A lot was at stake here, and they couldn't afford to fail. Not only were thousands of lives at stake, maybe even millions, but their two careers were also on the line. They simply had to succeed.

Jack said, "Nervous?"

"A little."

"This is not your first time for a firefight, so what's the issue here?"

"The stakes are higher than ever before, this is the first time so many lives depend on what we do here."

Jack thought about that, he'd faced situations like this before, but in the heat of the moment, all that mattered was that you didn't lose your cool and do something foolish that would get you or your partner killed. He said, "Don't think of it that way, or you'll freeze up. This is just another drug bust, so treat it like that, okay?"

She didn't have time to comment as they had arrived. The elevator stopped, and the doors opened.

CHAPTER THIRTY-SEVEN

Jack saw the first guard and went straight at him. A punch to the jaw took him down before he could raise the alarm.

They moved quickly inside. The elevator had deposited them in a short corridor that had three doors leading off it, one on either side and one at the far end.

Jack deduced that what they needed would be deep inside the facility, and the door at the far end would be the one they needed. The guard they had met when getting off the elevator would just be one of many. He would be the one guarding the entrance and probably reported any newcomers to those inside.

They made their way to the door and paused. As soon as they opened this door, the two of them knew there would be no turning back. In fact, they had reached that point the moment they entered the elevator.

Placing his hand on the door, Jack looked at Charley to see if she was ready. Her nod gave him the answer he was waiting for.

He opened the door and stepped through.

The room facing them was an open-plan laboratory. It had rows of desks with futuristic equipment adorned on them that Jack had never seen before. It looked like something out of a sci-fi movie, and he was feeling a little out of his depth.

"Any idea what any of this does?" he asked as he saw her looking around with a little more recognition than him.

"Not a fuckin' clue, you?" she replied with a smile.

"We need to find what Franklin was working on and hope the antidote is with it," Jack said, "but I have no clue what to look for."

"Perhaps we should ask them," Charley suggested looking away across the room. Jack followed her gaze to see what her eyes had landed on.

There was a group of four scientists hard at work at the far end of the room. Huddled around various pieces of equipment, they all had their heads down, so they were unaware of the two newcomers among them.

Two guards stood overlooking their work, and as Jack and Charley entered the room, they looked up.

Jack was the first to react. He brought up his pistol and fired. The first guard went down from the bullet to his chest.

As soon as the first shot was fired, pandemonium erupted in the room. Screams from the scientists working there filled the air, almost drowning out the sounds of gunfire.

The remaining guard opened fire on the two intruders, forcing them to dive behind desks for cover. Bullets struck the desk Jack was behind, sending sparks flying. Charley had gone in the opposite direction to him and peered around the side to return fire.

Jack saw that the scientists had all dropped behind

desks at the front of the room, fearful for their lives, cowering as low as they could. Jack saw his chance as the guard came up to fire at Charley. Jack quickly took aim and fired as soon as his target appeared from behind the tall piece of equipment he'd been hiding behind. His bullet hit him in the shoulder, spinning him around. His gun went off, firing indiscriminately into the ceiling as he fell.

Jack and Charley went forward through a gap in the row of desks. The last guard came up from the floor, and Jack shot him again, this time in the face. He dropped like a stone, his face obliterated by the gunshot.

The first guard was already dead from their initial encounter, which just left the scientists.

"You are quite safe now, no one will hurt you anymore," Jack said to the cowering group.

He saw their faces look up at him with a mixture of fear and relief.

"Where is the drug that Doctor Franklin was working on?" Charley asked. The urgency in her tone alerted them to the possibility of further danger.

One of them stood up, he was possibly the oldest, shorter than Jack, with thinning grey hair. When he spoke, he had a thin, reedy voice, "Franklin was working over here, all his records should be in the computer over there," he said.

Jack moved over to the computer mentioned, and the scientist logged on, opening it up. He searched for the document folder in question. Taking out his phone, he photographed each page with the device's camera. When he was sure he had everything he needed, he deleted the file from the computer.

"We have it all here, now all we have to do is get it to the right people," he told Charley.

Charley was just about to say something when Jack saw her eyes dart somewhere behind him. As he turned, he just had time to see three more guards appear, guns raised.

"Down!" Jack shouted as gunfire tore the silence apart.

"How do you plan to get what's on your phone to the right people now?" Charley asked him as the two of them hid behind the computer desk.

"I'm working on it," Jack replied.

CHAPTER THIRTY-EIGHT

Bullets ripped apart the top of the desk they were using as cover. The scientists had also dropped down behind other desks to get away from the onslaught, trying to distance themselves from these two intruders.

Jack peered around the side for a second to catch sight of the three newcomers. He fired around the side at the first person he saw. A scream of pain told him his aim had been true. He saw the guard drop to the floor from the gunshot to his leg, and another shot finished him off as the bullet smacked into his forehead ending his involvement.

"One down," he said.

Seeing one of their own die gave the other two caution, and they separated across the width of the room. Their intention was clear, to catch Jack and Charley in a crossfire.

Jack pointed out the direction in which they had gone to Charley, and she followed the one nearest to her with her eyes.

More gunfire peppered the desk. They intended to

keep their heads down until the shooters were in position. Jack waited for it to end, for when they had to reload, and then moved.

He fired over the top of the desk twice, then performed a combat roll out into the aisle, coming up on his haunches. He had a clear shot at his target and took it.

The shooter dropped like a stone from the impact of his gun going off from a reflex. A spray of shells passed over Jack's head as he fell to the floor.

Now he was out in the open. He was a target himself. In his peripheral vision, he saw the other shooter turn to take advantage of this sudden opportunity and aim his rifle at him. Jack saw death looking across at him down the barrel of a Heckler and Koch MP5 sub-machine pistol and knew there was nothing he could do. Bracing for the impact, he gritted his teeth, realizing his mistake.

A gunshot went off, and he blinked but felt nothing. Opening his eyes, he saw the gunman drop with a surprised look on his face.

To his right, he saw Charley bring up her gun, still aimed at the shooter. She had saved his life.

His look of relief said 'thank you', which earned him a smile from her that replied, 'you're welcome'.

"Let's get the hell out of here," she said as she came over to him.

"I agree. Before any more guards find their way down here."

He walked over to the scientists as they, too, were getting to their feet, a thought on his mind.

"Is there another route out of here, in case of fire or if there was a breach of containment, that sort of thing?" he asked the scientist he had spoken to earlier.

With a nod, the man said, "This way."

He led them out of the room and into a passageway that led deeper into the facility. They passed more doors which led to other parts of the underground structure, which Jack ignored but marked in his memory for future reference should it become relevant. At the end of the passageway was another door. The scientist opened it with a code and then walked through. Now they were in the basement. There were pipes trailing down the side of another passage that was lit by bulbs strung along the roof, giving off just enough illumination for them to see where they were going.

Jack recognized this area as a maintenance level, this would be where the heating and ventilation systems were housed.

They were led down a series of twists and turns until they came to a brick wall at the end. A ladder fastened to this led up to a hatch in the ceiling.

"Up there, this is the only other way out," the scientist said.

Jack looked at Charley, his suspicion narrowed his eyes.

"Wait here, and keep an eye on them," he said, indicating the group with them.

Holstering his pistol, he grabbed the ladder and started to climb. The hatch was opened by a simple bolt. He pushed the hatch back on its hinges and looked out. The passage had taken them out past the perimeter of the upper structure they had entered earlier. Looking around, he could see no one, so he climbed out. When he stood up, he could see the building and the chopper they had arrived in, not too far away.

"Okay, it's clear you can come up," he said to Charley, who was standing at the bottom of the ladder, sharing her concentration between keeping watch on the group of scientists and what was happening above.

At the top, Jack looked around for a means of travel. They needed to get away from here and fast but also without anyone seeing them.

The chopper was the obvious choice, but seeing as how they would see them leave, he was reluctant to take that chance.

What choice did he have though?

As the first of the small group got up to stand next to him, he leaned over the shaft to say, "Hurry up, we need to get moving and fast."

CHAPTER THIRTY-NINE

Quesada had been waiting for Harper to arrive, and when he was late, he called his mobile. After several rings, it went to voicemail, and he knew something had gone wrong.

Storming out of the villa, he searched the skies, listening for any signs that the chopper was heading their way.

Nothing.

Looking around as he patrolled the grounds, he came across a chopper parked near the annex.

"Mierda!" he snapped as he realized what had happened. As he watched, he saw a group of the scientists who had been working down in the lab run towards the chopper escorted by the two agents.

Taking out his pistol, he opened fire on them.

———

Jack heard gunfire and saw one of their group go down, blood pooling beneath his head. Shot, and he knew the man was dead without the need to check.

Instinctively the rest of them all went into a crouch when the gunfire went off. Jack turned in the direction it was coming from and saw a large man standing, firing a handgun at them.

It would take seconds before others came and joined him, so their need to escape had just reached the desperate stage.

"Get them inside the chopper," he shouted to Charley, then took out his own gun and returned fire. The slide locked back as the last round exited the chamber, and he ejected the clip. Taking a fresh one from inside his jacket, he inserted it into the butt, pulled back on the slide to inject a fresh round into the breach, and he was good to go, all within a few seconds.

His next two shots made the shooter think twice about remaining where he stood. He saw him move as one of his bullets almost creased his head, and he ran for cover, firing over his shoulder, crouching low.

Jack quickly climbed aboard the chopper and started the engines. He had them warmed up just in time to see more armed guards emerge to fire at them with automatic weapons.

Charley was in the seat next to him, staring out the window and returning fire as best she could.

"This would be a really good time to go, Jack," she screamed at him over the noise of the engines and gunfire.

"I'm working on it," he replied as he pulled back on the cyclic and collective. He boosted power to the engines, and they were in the air. As soon as they were off the ground, he moved the chopper in a tight turn away from the shooters, and they were off, increasing speed with every second and climbing into the air at the same time.

The gunfire drifted off back into the distance behind them, and both Jack and Charley let out a sigh.

"I think we made it, man," she said to him, smiling.

Jack was unconvinced, there was a lot at stake here for Moya, and he doubted he would leave it at that.

Quesada was fuming. He lashed out at his men snarling at them, "Get the chopper! They cannot escape."

He ran with them to the other chopper, and the pilot was spooling up the engines. It was soon in the air, giving chase. Quesada was in one open doorway with two of the others hanging out of the opposite door, all bearing assault rifles.

They were a hunting party, and Jack and Charley were the prey.

Jack took out his phone and called HQ.

"I'm sending you a series of photos. Get them analyzed as fast as you can, it may hold the key to fighting this drug. With a bit of luck, it could hold the antidote as well," he said before anything could be said.

He quickly sent the photos through and returned the phone to his ear.

"We're on our way home now," he finished off, then closed the call returning his phone to his pocket.

"You don't sound convinced," Charley observed.

As if in reply to that, bullets hammered the rear of the chopper.

Jack turned the controls to the left, sending the craft away from the gunfire.

"Hang on back there, this is going to get a little bumpy," Jack said to the scientists in the rear compartment.

He swerved through the sky, dodging and weaving as gunfire chased them through the sky.

The hull of the craft sustained a few hits as the engine was targeted.

"We can't carry on like this. Before long, they'll hit something vital, and then you know what happens," Charley said, peering through the door at the chasing chopper.

"I'm working on it," Jack replied, but deep down, he knew she was right. Unless they could shake their tail, it was just a matter of time before they caught up with them and inflicted enough damage to bring them down.

"Try and persuade them not to shoot at us," he suggested.

Charley glanced his way, her eyes going wide as she asked, "And how the fuck do you suggest I do that?"

"Shoot back, perhaps?" he said without looking at her. His concentration was on trying to keep their chopper from being hit by the gunfire from behind.

With a grunt, Charley leaned out of the window with her gun outstretched and fired at the following chopper.

Jack saw it swerve out of the way and then swing around for another attacking run.

Sending their chopper low into the ground, Jack tried to lose them as he headed for some rolling hills that had deep valleys in between. With a bit of luck, he hoped their pilot wasn't as brave as he seemed and would back off.

The terrain looped around to the right with grass-covered hills to their left and right that seemed to roll on forever. He dipped the chopper low to get as close to the ground as he could.

Bullets zinged past them as the following chopper didn't give up the chase, but Jack noticed the shots were lessening. The terrain was clearly causing them more problems than they expected.

"What the fuck are you doing?" Charley asked as she noticed their speed bleed off.

"Giving you a better chance at hitting your damn target, now don't let me down."

He allowed the chasing chopper to gain air on them and hoped Charley was as good a shot as he needed her to be.

"Get ready," he said.

At the last second, he spun the chopper to the left, going broadside onto the onrushing aircraft and giving Charley a clear shot.

Looking past her through the open door, he clearly saw the look of surprise on the pilot's face, his eyes went wide as saucers as he saw the gun aimed right at him.

Charley emptied her clip into the pilot's cabin, keeping each shot as tightly grouped as she could under the circumstances. Then, as her slide locked back, Jack turned their craft in a tight turndown and away from the other chopper.

He had seen the bullet strikes on the Plexiglass window of the chopper and saw the pilot react, dancing as at least three of the bullets hit him center mass. As he guided the chopper back on an even flight path, he knew the other aircraft would be in a dire state. With the pilot hit, they would lose control and fall quickly out of the sky. If no one took over the controls, they were certainly going to crash.

The chopper dipped out of sight, and neither Jack nor Charley could see where it went until an explosion was heard from somewhere behind them.

"I think we lost 'em," Charley told him, sitting back around to face the front once more.

Jack was relieved, "Let's go home."

————

Quesada saw the pilot get hit as the chopper turned sideways onto them. They would have crashed into them had it not been for the pilot's quick reactions.

Three times he was hit in the chest, then he slumped forward, and there was no need to check, he knew he was dead.

The chopper went into a tailspin toward the ground. They were so close, fear gripped his innards. He had faced death many times in his life, staring it down, and this would be no different. He pushed the pilot through the door and took the controls as they plummeted towards certain death below.

He had watched the pilot on many occasions, so he knew a little about flying. He grabbed both controls and stamped on the pedals hoping that he was doing the right thing.

The chopper continued down until whatever he was doing finally brought their speed down, but they saw the ground coming up too fast. He managed to level it off, the rotors desperately trying to grab more air to give them the lift they so needed.

The bottom of the chopper slammed into the ground,

breaking up on impact as they spun out of control. It tilted over as it slid across the moisture-laden grass, and then the rotors hit the ground, snapping off and spinning high into the air across the open space.

The passengers were thrown around inside as they frantically attempted to grab hold of anything to stabilize themselves.

Quesada was thrown clear as the chopper continued its frantic journey across the valley until a stray spark ignited the leaking fuel. The explosion ripped apart what was left of the aircraft killing those inside instantly.

Quesada held his hands over his head and pressed himself into the ground as the shockwave passed over him.

Breathing deeply, he staggered to his feet as flaming debris rained down from above.

He turned to look at where his target was flying, disappearing from sight, and swore a silent oath that he would avenge the deaths of his men when he finally caught up with the two agents.

Taking out his mobile, he called Moya to let him know of his failure.

———

Back at the villa, Moya was enraged by the news.

How was it possible for them to escape again?

He had sent a truck to pick up Quesada and stopped pacing the width of his lounge when he heard the sound of engines. Something made him stop when he heard them, these were not the sound of a truck, more like a chopper's engine, and it was coming in fast.

Explosions ripped the house front off as rockets struck the building, throwing Moya into total confusion.

Was another competitor taking the opportunity to attack him like the last time?

Clambering over rubble, he looked through the destroyed front of his beloved home and saw the chopper as it hovered, taking aim once more, an Apache attack helicopter.

Those damned Federales had grown some balls and decided to take him on. He thought when he saw no markings on the side of the craft.

More explosions destroyed parts of the villa, and as he saw his troops come out to defend his home, they were mercilessly cut down by the cannons slung beneath the attack chopper. Bodies were chopped into bloody pieces by the fifty-caliber shells fired from the chopper, making Moya even angrier.

The truck sent to pick up Quesada skidded to a halt in the drive beneath the chopper, and he saw his friend beckon him forward to it.

Desperately looking for a way out, he ran through the villa and exited through a side door, then sprinted to the edge of the drive as the chopper continued its attack.

He managed to climb aboard the truck without being seen, and it was soon driving away from the damaged property.

"Who was that?" Quesada asked as he peered through the back window to see the chopper finish off the villa with more rockets and cannon fire. There was no chance that anyone could survive that onslaught.

"I don't know, but I have an idea it could have something to do with those meddling agents Harper was supposed to have brought to me," Moya replied angrily.

"What happened to him?" he asked Quesada.

"They must have overpowered him somehow and then found the scientists below the annex. I saw them leaving with some of them. That was who I was chasing before they managed to escape again," Quesada replied sheepishly.

Whoever they are, wherever they went, they will rue the day they decided to interfere with my affairs," Moya swore.

"What do you intend to do, Patron?"

"We will follow them and kill them and everyone they care about," he said.

He sat back, his face cold and hard as he thought about the time he looked into their eyes just before he placed a bullet in each of their brains.

CHAPTER FORTY

SECTION ZERO HQ—AUGUST 27

By the time Jack and Charley returned to England, the photos he had sent through had been with them long enough for them to be analyzed.

After landing at Fairfax, the two agents returned to Section Zero, hoping to hear some good news. Time was running out for all those infected in Miami, they only had hours left before they started dying.

"Tell me you found something," Jack said when he saw Tony in the corridor. He looked to be coming back from somewhere too.

"We had the photos looked at and analyzed, and we found what Franklin had manufactured," Tony replied. "Good work over there, by the way. Both of you did remarkably well."

"Thanks, but did you find an antidote amongst all that research?" Jack asked. The urgency in his voice hinted at the anguish he felt, which was mirrored in his expression.

Charley placed a comforting hand on his arm before speaking, "Give the man a chance to explain."

Tony gave her a nod of appreciation. "We did, and we passed our intel over to the DEA. It's up to them to implement it now, it's out of our hands."

"So the threat to other countries is now eliminated?" Charley posited.

"Nice to see you all got back safely," Bennett said as they entered his office. The particular way that sentence was formed did not go unnoticed by Jack, who looked at Tony for confirmation. His blank expression said more than words ever could.

"You just got back too, Colonel? Where from?" Jack asked.

Before Tony could reply, Bennett said, "We just got word from the US that Moya's villa has been destroyed. A preliminary investigation has shown there were no survivors, but so far, they have not found his body."

This got both Jack and Charley's full attention. They looked intensely at Bennett, and Jack asked for both of them, "Excuse me, destroyed? When did that happen?"

All eyes turned to Tony, who shrugged his shoulders, "I'm as much in the dark as everyone else here."

"Quite," Bennett said, then continued, "The Americans deny any involvement in the attack, so I can only imagine it was someone with a vested interest in seeing the Moya Cartel put out of business."

Jack glanced at the Colonel when he said, "Whoever it was, I'd like to shake his hand."

"Well, for the time being, things are out of our hands. The Americans will distribute the antidote to Franklin's drug cocktail, and things should return to normal pretty soon. Of course, they will claim all the credit for this operation, which sticks in my craw somewhat, but it is what it is. The main thing is we saved millions of lives, so I can live with them taking the glory," Bennett said.

He looked at the three of them and gave a little smile.

"Thanks to you three, the first operation of Section Zero has been a success, and I must warn you, Agent Parker, that anything you learned here and or took part in must stay on the official record, which means, as I'm sure you're aware of, no one can learn of your, or our participation in any of this. I have squared your involvement away with your superiors so there will be no backlash from them. Things will fall heavily on the shoulders of the Agent in Charge, Bill Harper. Now if I were you, all of you, I would take a few days off to rest. You've earned it."

"You don't have to tell me twice, sir. I have a new place to move into and finalize, so time off is just what I need," Jack said. He turned to Tony, held out a hand to shake, then said, "See you soon, Colonel."

Tony gave his hand a firm shake, then replied with a wink, "See you soon, Jack."

Charley followed Jack through the door, and he said, "If you aren't in a rush to get back, we could grab that drink."

Smiling, she said, "I'd like that."

The two of them left to go to the car park where Jack had parked his car. Now they could relax and get to know each other properly, although, after what they had been through together this last couple of days, Jack was certain there wasn't much he didn't know about her. Situations of high tension, such as combat, brought out the best and worst in people. It was at times like those that you saw their true personality emerge. In Charley's case, Jack liked what he'd seen and wanted to see more.

The look she had given him when she accepted his offer of a drink told him she felt the same about him.

CHAPTER FORTY-ONE

LONDON—AUGUST 30

The Grand Hotel in Trafalgar Square in London was a boutique hotel that catered for any taste. It had all the amenities a hotel in the center of London was expected to have. From a fitness center to a conference room, it somehow blended the old with the new inside a historic building.

Moya noticed none of this as he had booked in and been shown up to his Superior Room on the third floor.

The room had a king-sized bed set against the wall with a desk opposite and a 22-inch smart TV fitted on a bracket against the wall. It also had tea and coffee-making facilities with a small fridge where the open bar was situated. Next to the door, as he entered, he noticed another door that led to the bathroom, fitted with a toilet, a large shower, and a sink.

It was more than adequate for his needs. He had wanted to be in a central London location while he finished his business with those meddling agents, but he didn't want to be too ostentatious.

After making sure he was alone, he took out his phone and called Quesada.

"Is everything in place?"

"I have the best hackers working on locating where the agents went, Patron, but so far, they have drawn a blank on the British agent."

"What about the female, the DEA agent? Can you find her at least?" Moya asked. He was getting impatient with this search, it was taking too long. Whoever this British agent was, he was well hidden.

"They have her located. She returned to the States two days ago," Quesada replied.

"Get hold of her and bring her here. We can tease him out of hiding. When he hears we have her, he won't be able to stop himself from trying to save her. These Western types are all the same, always wanting to play the hero. When he finds out we have her, we can get him to meet us wherever we want, and then..." Moya said, trailing off the sentence.

"Then what, Patron?" Quesada asked, playing along.

"...then we kill them both."

———

CHARLOTTE, NORTH CAROLINA, US

Charley was just recovering from her recent ordeal and beginning to feel more like her old self again.

Since returning to the States, she had been debriefed by the regional head of the DEA, who had then given her two weeks' leave. From there, she went home to Charlotte. She had popped in to see her family to ensure they were alright, then went back to the apartment she rented.

It was a small place with a single bedroom, a bathroom, and a kitchen/lounge set up. She didn't plan on staying there too long, just until she knew what was happening with her parents.

She had always planned on starting a family by the time she was thirty-five with a career firmly established, but seeing as how she was still trying to make her mark in the DEA and her thirtieth birthday had already come and gone, things were not looking too good on that front.

Then she found herself thinking of Jack Cross and their time together, and despite the danger they both faced, how much she had enjoyed his company. She had his number...should she give him a call, she wondered?

Dismissing that thought, she went to the bathroom to run a shower. She had no plans for the evening, so she decided to take a shower, climb into her comfy clothes and settle down for the night with a good book. She'd picked up a copy of *Pray for Death* by a new British author by the name of Jack Dillon. She hadn't seen any of his work before, so she had thought, why not, and took it home. It wasn't until she got it home she realized it was book three in a series, but she thought, what the hell, she would read it anyway.

Just as she was reaching for a fresh towel to take in with her, the doorbell rang.

"Who the hell can this be?" she said to herself, then stopped. No one knew what her address was outside of the DEA.

Walking over to the nightstand, she retrieved her service weapon, jacked the slide as silently as she could, and held it at her side as she walked slowly to her door.

Standing in front of the door, she said loudly, "Who is it?" then quickly moved to the side, pressing her back to the wall adjacent to the door.

"I have some mail of yours here, it was delivered to me by mistake," a friendly voice said.

"Just post it through the letterbox, please," she replied calmly.

"I can't do that, it's too big to go through the slot."

Now she knew something was up.

Her adrenaline spiked as she wondered who it could be and how many of them there were. Undoubtedly, they would be armed, and she had only one gun.

They would have all the exits covered, and there was no other way down from here, so she had no choice but to open the door.

Tucking her pistol into the waistband of her jeans at the small of her back beneath her white blouse, she said, "Okay, give me a sec' and I'll be right there."

She unlocked the door and pulled it open.

The first thing she saw was the muzzle of a pistol being pointed at her face.

No suppressor, this was good news, it meant they wanted her alive. If they wanted her dead, they could've shot her through the door when she stepped to open it.

Acting quickly, she grabbed the hand holding the pistol and pulled the man towards her, then twisted at the last second, performing a hip toss to throw the shooter over her to the ground. As she did that, she kicked the door shut, slamming it in the face of the second man. Still having hold of the weapon in one hand, she punched the man in the face with her other hand. His head hit the floor, and the double impact stunned him.

She stepped past his body as the door was kicked

open, slamming it against the wall. This allowed the other two men to join the fight.

Determined not to go out without a fight, she reached for her gun.

Both men had entered with their guns raised, but she hoped taking her alive would prevent them from shooting her first.

She quickly aimed at the first as the two men separated and fired two bullets. Her shots hit center mass, sending him to the floor in a grimace of pain, but before she could reposition her aim, the third man had closed the gap between them and was pressing his pistol hard against her head.

"Drop the gun, chica," he said in a thick Mexican accent.

"I would do as he says, Agent Parker. It is not your time to die. Not today, at least," another voice said as the owner of that voice strode confidently into the room.

Through the corner of her eye, she saw who it was.

"Quesada. Where's your boss, Moya?" she said.

"Oh, don't worry, you'll see him soon enough, chica. Now I don't suppose you'd like to save us some time and a whole lot of trouble for you and tell me the name of the other agent who was with you," Quesada said as he came to stand in front of her, looking down at her.

"I don't know what you're talkin' about."

"I thought not," he said, looking around. He saw what he wanted, walked over to the couch, and picked up her phone. He grabbed her hand and placed her finger on the scanner to open it and then began scrolling through her call list. Some he recognized, some he didn't, but the one that interested him was one brief contact made a few days ago.

He looked into her eyes and smiled.

"Never mind, chica, I have what I want."

CHAPTER FORTY-TWO

LONDON—AUGUST 30

Jack looked around his apartment, things were beginning to take shape. Most of his things had been unpacked, and the furniture put in place. There were just some things he couldn't bring himself to either dispose of or even unpack, things that belonged to his wife and daughter.

There was one thing that had pride of place by his bedside, and that was a picture of the three of them together. It would have been one of the last times they did anything as a family before his last return to SI6.

He had placed it next to his lamp at the side of his bed so it would be the last thing he saw before turning out the light and the first thing he saw in the morning.

Until the move had begun, he hadn't known how much was involved in moving home. He had read somewhere that moving home, changing jobs, and a death in the family were three of the top five most stressful things you had to face in your life. He had faced all three in one go, no wonder he was tired. Although, strictly speaking, he hadn't actually changed jobs, his job had changed in the respect that he had new bosses and a new place of work, but the job description and what he did for a living hadn't changed that much, but that was just semantics.

There were still a few things he needed for the apartment, so he had eaten his breakfast and was wondering where the place would be to get them when his phone rang. He recognized the ID straight away, which brought a smile to his face.

He pressed 'answer' and said, "What's up, Charley, missing me already?"

"Cute, you have feelings for her. I like that. If you want to save her, you will do as I say, no questions asked, do you understand?" a voice with a heavy accent said.

"Who is this, and what have you done with Charley?" Jack asked, his voice dropping an octave as anger flooded his system. If they had harmed her because of his involvement, they would surely pay, but he couldn't think of that just yet.

"Who I am is of no importance, that I have Miss Parker is. If you want to see no harm come to her, you will come to Charlotte right away, alone."

"And if I refuse?"

"You won't because you consider yourself the hero in this little story of ours. Allowing her to die goes against everything you hold dear, so you will come, and you will do as you are told, willingly, I might add."

"If you harm her—" Jack started to say but was cut off immediately.

"You are in no position to bargain or threaten. You have no control here, I am in control. Come to Charlotte. When you arrive, you will receive further instructions on where to go."

Jack wanted to say more, but the call ended abruptly.

He got the impression that at the end, the caller was beginning to lose it slightly. He also got the impression that, whoever the caller was, he was the type of man accustomed to getting what he wanted and not used to people saying 'no' to him.

Felix Moya, it had to be him. So, he *had* survived the attack on his villa. The damned man had more lives than a cat.

Activating the secure function on his coded mobile, he called HQ.

When the call was answered, he asked to be put through to Bennett.

"Listen, sir, I don't have a great deal of time. I've just received a call on Agent Parker's phone from who I think is Felix Moya. He has summoned me to a meeting in Charlotte, but I doubt that'll be the final destination. He probably wants to give me the runaround, have me running all over the place to ensure I'm not being followed. If I don't go, he has assured me he will kill Agent Parker. I am to go alone, obviously," he said quickly.

"I suppose he'll give you further instructions on your arrival?"

"Yes, sir."

"That seems to confirm your theory. Is there the slightest chance Agent Parker could be working for Moya?" Bennett asked.

"No, sir, I would stake my life on it."

"You are."

"I suppose I am. I just thought you should know, sir. I'm leaving for the airport now. I'll catch the first available flight."

"You'll do no such thing," Bennett told him.

"Sir?"

"You'll get yourself off to Fairfax and take the Gulf-stream. I'll see what I can do to arrange some backup for you, but I can't guarantee anything, you understand."

"That's alright, sir. I think I may know someone who could help out in a pinch, and thanks for the lift. I'll give you an update when I arrive, sir," Jack said and ended the call.

At the mention of 'backup', an idea suddenly sprung to his mind, and he smiled.

As he grabbed what he needed for the trip, he exited his apartment and headed for the garage where he'd left his car. As he set off for Fairfax, he rang the number of the person he thought might be able to help. When the phone was answered, he said, "Mike, I may need your assistance, buddy, and it involves Charley. She's in a spot of bother, and I'm going to help."

Mike Flynn said, "Tell me what you need, Buddy."

CHAPTER FORTY-THREE

CHARLOTTE, NC, USA—AUGUST 30

Jack exited the plane after landing at Charlotte Douglas International Airport and got in the car that was waiting for him. The airport was only eight miles from Charlotte, so he figured he would be there in no time, so he called Charley's phone to get new instructions.

The same voice answered his call and gave an address with a time he had to arrive and then rang off, not giving him time to comment or argue. Clearly, Moya wanted to remain in control of the situation and seemed to be enjoying himself.

Using the Pay-as-You-Go phone he had bought en route to Fairfax, he called Mike.

"On my way to the rendezvous now. I'll text you the address in a sec. Are you set?"

Mike's voice came through as clear as ever, and he seemed more like his old self when he said, "I'm all set to go, buddy. Don't you worry, I've got your back."

"It'll be just like old times, my friend. See you there," Jack said.

"No, you won't," Mike replied before ending the call. Jack wasn't worried, he knew exactly what Mike had meant. If he saw him, then he'd failed, and they would both end up being killed.

He sent the address via a text using the throwaway phone, and it immediately rang. It was Mike.

"Buddy, that address is a private airfield. If Moya's idea is to get you on a chopper or a small jet, then you'll be on your own, there's no way I can organize a ride to follow you, and I wouldn't know where to go anyway."

"I have an idea where he'll be taking me, to somewhere he'll feel completely in control, and that has to be somewhere in Columbia," Jack said as a feeling of dread sank deep into his stomach.

"Buddy, I don't know what to say. I'll call Tony in England to give him a sit-rep once I know for sure you've taken off. I'll see if a flight plan has been logged so I can let them know where you're going," Mike said.

"There's nothing you can do, Mike. Don't get involved in this. It could ruin your career if you try to follow me. Just let them know back in the UK that I'll take out Moya, once and for all."

He was truly on his own, which was brought more into focus when he arrived at the given address. It was, as Mike had told him, a private airfield. He entered through a steel mesh gate attached to a wire fence that ran around the perimeter of the airfield. It had one runway and a small control tower, nothing more than a tin hut, really. On the tarmac was a chopper with the pilot already getting the engine warmed up and ready for take-off. At the side stood two men holding pistols close to their chests, they were to be his escort on the final part of his journey.

He parked up next to the chopper, got out, and walked over to the men who waved him aboard. Each man had the blank stare and dead expression of the professional mercenary, part of Moya's Sicario team.

Knowing this was probably the last journey he would ever take, he got in and settled down, strapping himself in. Whatever happened after this, he was determined he would kill Felix Moya first.

———

SECTION ZERO HQ

Tony picked up his phone on the first ring. He had recognized the ID and was expecting the call.

"Mike, good to hear from you. What do you have?" he said, cutting through the preliminaries.

"I've just left Jack at a private airfield. He took off in a chopper with two men as guards. Both of us think he's being taken to Moya somewhere in Columbia, but it could be anywhere. There are thousands of places where bodies have been dumped, he could be going to any of them."

"Thanks. Are you heading home now?"

"Yes, there's nothing more I can do here. I can't follow as I have no idea where he's being taken."

"I'll pass on what you just told me, and I'll let you know as soon as we hear anything," Tony said, then hung up. He had to get this latest news to Bennett, who suddenly appeared in his doorway.

"Mike Flynn, I presume," he said. "I had an idea Cross would contact him. What did he say?"

Tony filled him in on what he'd been said and saw Bennett's eyes go wide as if something had occurred to him.

"We may not be able to help Cross and Agent Parker, but there may be another way," he said and turned to leave.

Tony was about to ask him, but his boss had already left.

Another way? What could he possibly have meant?

CHAPTER FORTY-FOUR

COLUMBIA

Jack sat looking out the window as the chopper approached a villa below. As soon as he saw it, he knew exactly where he was.

Moya's villa, his home. He supposed, in the drug lord's mind, this would be a fitting end to this situation. After all, it had all begun here, why not let it end here too.

Several men appeared from the ruins of the once proud home of one of the largest drug cartels in Columbia. He recognized Moya and the brute standing next to him, and there were three others, all armed with assault rifles.

Whatever he had planned for him, Moya was making certain he had enough firepower to ensure it wasn't disrupted this time.

Adrenaline flooded his system as he knew they were in the endgame now. Breathing slowly, he tried to keep his body under control. He couldn't allow panic to take over his actions now. He had to remain calm, keep a clear head, and be ready to make his move when the opportunity arose.

The chopper landed, and the door was opened by one of the guards on the ground while the other two aimed their rifles at him. They were taking no chances this time where he was concerned.

"Where is she?" he asked before he took one step from the chopper.

"Glad you could make it. You have me at a disadvantage though. You know who I am, but I know next to nothing about you. All I do know is that you're a British agent, oh and another thing, that you have feelings for Agent Parker," Moya said, standing with his feet shoulder-width apart and his arms folded across his chest.

"That's right," Jack agreed.

"Which part?" Moya wanted to know.

"You know next to nothing."

Moya smiled, "I like you, you have balls. Let's see just how big they are when we're done." The smile disappeared, leaving nothing but a cold hard stare.

Jack returned the stare giving him nothing, showing no sign of weakness.

"Take him inside," Moya said.

The two men who had rifles trained on him urged him forward.

He had to find out where Charley was being held, and that was never going to happen with him standing there. He moved towards the villa as the two men separated, flanking him, keeping their rifles aimed at him all the time.

He walked slowly to the villa while Moya remained where he stood, watching. Jack kept his eyes firmly planted on Moya's, never deviating an inch. The man standing at Moya's shoulder seemed to loom over him; his shoulders appeared so wide he would have to turn sideways to enter a room. His face seemed to have been carved from granite with a hammer, and Jack knew him to be a brutal fighter. This one had to be his top minder.

The villa had been attacked again, and the Destruction was evident everywhere.

"Love what you've done to the place," Jack taunted.

The brute stepped forward to block his path.

"You think you're a tough guy? Laugh in the face of danger and all that bullshit. Well, that's good. I like a sense of humor. Let's see if you still have that when we're done with you and the little lady in there," Quesada said.

Jack looked him in the eye, he was a little taller than him, so he had to look down just a little. The minder was broader and built like a pro wrestler with thick arms and legs.

Jack gave him a wink, "Go for it."

Moya, who had now joined them, said, "I like him even more. It'll be fun to watch him being taken apart before we kill him and his little lady friend."

Jack let it go. He would allow them to think they had him where they wanted, and to some degree, they had. He would play their game and play nice until it was time to turn nasty. When that happened, they would know they had messed with the wrong man.

CHAPTER FORTY-FIVE

The villa was a mess again. As Jack was shown inside, they moved him toward the rear of the building.

There was a door at the back near the kitchen that led down to a cellar. Jack guessed it was the wine cellar and was where they were holding Charley.

One of the guards went first while the other followed Jack down the narrow stairs. There were light bulbs in fittings down the side of the walls giving just enough light to see where they were going. At the bottom, the room opened out, and he saw rows of wooden wine racks filling the floor.

Overhead lights illuminated the large, low-ceilinged room, throwing long shadows across the floor. As the room opened out at the edge of where the wine racks ended, he could see three support beams holding up the ceiling. Charley was standing in front of one of these with her hands tied firmly behind her back and around the vertical beam.

Her expression when she saw him was a mix of relief

and sadness. Relief that he was safe and sadness that he, too, was now in the same situation as her.

Moya came down after him and walked around him to stand between the two of them.

"Isn't this nice, a reunion. Be glad to see each other because the games are about to begin."

Jack glanced at him and saw his minder standing beside him give him a smile that was full of evil intent.

Moya raised his hand to speak when a loud noise made them all freeze.

Jack saw a shiver of fear run through Moya as he heard the sound. He turned to his minder, his eyes wide.

"What the fuck is happening?"

Jack had no idea what caused what sounded like an explosion. He had thought he was on his own, no backup available, but this could just be the opportunity he needed.

The minder took off up the stairs to see what was going on. Jack waited for him to leave; he was obviously the most dangerous of all Moya's men present, and he would deal with him later.

The tension in the room had spiked through the ceiling with the first noise. Gunfire ripped through the silence, giving them all a better impression of what was happening.

The villa was under attack, again.

The guards were looking around, wondering what to do, and Jack saw his chance.

One of the guards was in front, and the other had come to stand near him, breaking protocol.

Jack moved fast.

He stepped forward and grabbed the barrel of the man on his left with his left hand and punched him squarely in the face with his right. The guard's grip on the weapon was loosened, enabling Jack to rip it from his grasp. Turning, he smashed the point of his elbow into the face of the second guard snapping his head back. Bullets peppered the wine rack to the side as he fired off a few rounds. Jack turned the rifle he had taken from the first guard on the second and fired a three-shot burst sending him crashing into the wine rack.

At the first sign of trouble, Moya ran for the stairs taking them three at a time until he cleared them and went back into the kitchen.

Jack snarled when he saw Moya escape, but he went to Charley to untie her.

"What kept you?" she asked, smiling.

"Traffic was terrible," he responded, returning the smile. As her hands were freed, she reached up with both hands, grabbed Jack's face, then planted a kiss firmly on his lips.

When they separated, he said, "Let's get the hell out of here, then you can thank me properly."

"That's a date."

The two of them searched the dead bodies for weapons. They each found a Glock and then took the discarded rifles and headed for the stairs.

At the bottom, Charley grabbed his arm.

"Who the hell is up there; who did you bring as back-up?" she asked.

Shaking his head, Jack said, "I came alone."

"Okay, well, they seem to be on our side, so what say we go join the party?"

Jack nodded his approval, and they set off up the stone stairs.

Emerging into the kitchen, they kept their rifles up at their shoulders, ready to fire.

Jack went right as Charley went left to cover their flanks.

Gunfire could be heard from the outside, which was echoed by more gunfire from inside the building.

Jack aimed at the first guard he saw and fired. A three-shot burst ended his participation in this. Charley fired on another, killing him too.

An open piece of floor was free, and they ran towards the front of the villa.

Moya was nowhere to be seen.

Jack caught a glimpse of someone running up the broad staircase to the upper floors.

He turned and placed a hand on Charley's shoulder. "Try and find us a ride out of here. I'm going after Moya."

Before she could argue, he was gone, running towards the staircase.

At the top of the staircase, the landing ran around the top floor with doors to every bedroom and bathroom along it. Jack saw a door slam shut and headed in that direction. At the top, he stopped outside the door to slow his breathing, then lashed out with his foot. The door slammed against the wall as it burst open.

At the far wall, Moya stood looking at a wall-mounted rack of guns.

"Moya, it's over," he shouted.

Moya spun around, holding a rifle from the rack, but before he could even aim it, Jack put three rounds in his chest, sending him crashing back against the rack.

Jack placed two fingers against Moya's carotid artery to check if his work was done. He got to his feet and left the bedroom, heading back downstairs. Part of the mission was complete. All that was left was to get the fuck out.

CHAPTER FORTY-SIX

Charley made her way to the front of the villa. Gunfire ripped apart furniture in front of her, causing her to duck beneath it for cover.

More bullets slammed into the thick sofa sending feathers and stuffing flying into the air with every hit.

She waited for a lull in the firing, then when it stopped, she got up, already having made a fix on where her target was, then fired a three-round burst in that direction.

A satisfying scream told her that her aim was true. Getting up, she made her way around the sofa and headed for an exit. Keeping her concentration focused on what was happening before her, she saw more of Moya's men defending the villa. She counted four, with at least as many lying bleeding or dead on the floor.

The closer she got to the front of the villa she could see through the opening exactly who was instigating the attack.

Several men dressed in normal clothes using assault rifles were circling the building hiding behind trucks and other vehicles. She counted at least eight men. She recognized them as Sicario, Columbian Cartel hitmen.

Someone must have warned the other cartels of Moya returning to his villa, and they sent out a team to finish the job. After what he had done to destroy the cartels and bring them all under his control, it made sense they would retaliate when he was down.

Unfortunately, they could be caught in the crossfire, but if they could commandeer one of the vehicles, they may be able to escape this mayhem.

Moving to the side, she saw one that might do the trick. It was an SUV parked at the side of the building, away from all the action at the moment, and it looked to be deserted.

There was a door at the side of the villa leading to a path that ran around the building and to the gardens at the back. The door was in front of her, and she kept low to avoid getting shot by the invading force. Reaching out to grab the door handle, she was suddenly grabbed from behind.

A massive arm suddenly wrapped around her throat, and in seconds her airwaves were constricted. Her air supply was cut off so swiftly and completely that she found her vision blurring in just a few seconds.

Struggling to breathe, she clutched at the arm, ripping and tearing at it in a vain attempt to pull it free, but it remained fast, immovable.

A hand was placed on the back of her head, pushing it onto the arm to increase the pressure on her throat.

Her struggles weakened as her lungs ached to find breath; her arms fell as darkness shrouded her vision, and as it filled her vision, her last thought before she blacked out was that Jack wouldn't save her this time.

———

Quesada tossed Charley over his massive shoulder like she weighed nothing. He had seen her approach as he hid in the shadows, watching who was attacking the villa, just waiting to make his move.

He saw her approach, keeping her head down, and he smiled. He never thought they would be able to escape, but it seems he had underestimated them, again. It would not happen again.

She would be used as bait once more, but this time he would take the Brit out at the first opportunity.

He would not escape this time.

———

Jack reached the bottom of the stairs and headed for the lounge area.

Gunfire rang out as he got closer to the front of the building. Several gunmen were fighting to protect the villa, and he wondered if they would fight so vociferously if they knew Moya was dead.

As he leveled his assault rifle up to his shoulder, he aimed at one of the men and fired, dropping him.

Heads turned in his direction to see where the shot had originated from, and he dropped two more.

The rest took cover, thrown into panic mode as they faced gunfire from both front and back now.

From the side, he caught a glimpse of a figure carrying something over his shoulder and realized what it was.

The minder, and he had Charley with him.

Somehow he had overpowered her and was taking her with him.

The moment he had laid eyes on the brute, he had

known there would be a reckoning between the two of them.

As fast as he could, he aimed and fired in his direction, aiming for the doorway he was heading for just to warn him.

The bullets struck the wood close to the brute's head, and he flinched slightly, stopping dead in his tracks.

He turned to face Jack, tossing the body of Charley to the ground.

Jack's anger flared momentarily, but he soon had it under control once more. He had seen Charley breathing, so he knew she was alive at least.

"Are you going to shoot me, agent-man?" the minder asked, smiling broadly at Jack.

Jack kept his assault rifle trained on him as he slowly walked toward him.

Slowly his finger squeezed the trigger, it would be over soon, and they could leave. A few more pounds of pressure on the trigger and the brute would be as dead as the man he worked for.

A salvo of gunfire went past his ear. He felt the air heat up as the hot shells burned their way past him. Involuntarily he flinched, taking his eye off the minder who closed the gap between them in a few fast strides.

Jack was tackled, and the two of them went tumbling to the ground.

The rifle went scattering across the floor, and he was pinned beneath the massive weight of the minder. He was stronger than Jack, and he had him at his mercy, but he was not about to give up.

Reaching up, he jabbed a thumb in the minder's right eye.

Quesada reared up from the pain in his eye. The last thing he wanted was to go blind in one eye. Jack was able to kick his way free the moment the brute released him.

He spun away and was on his feet, facing his adversary once more.

Just as he got ready, the big man charged him again. Huge arms grabbed him around the waist as a rock-hard shoulder slammed into his midriff. Jack was hoisted off the ground as the minder charged him, and when he stopped, Jack felt the arms change their hold on him as he was slammed back to the ground at the minder's feet.

Jack thought his back had broken from the impact as all the air in his lungs was forced out in a loud 'whoosh!'

Acting purely on instinct, he lashed out with both feet at the man standing over him. He felt a satisfying crunch as they struck his face, allowing him the time to flip himself back onto his feet.

Jack struck the already damaged face with a series of jabs, then a thunderous right cross that just turned the rock-like head to the side. Quesada turned back to look at Jack and smiled.

"That all you got, Gringo?"

Quesada went on the attack again, swinging blows at Jack's head, which he either ducked under or dodged.

Jack blocked a roundhouse right fist with a double-handed block, then struck his attacker with a back-fist that rocked his face around.

Carrying on with his attack Jack struck him again with a left cross, then a right blow to the throat.

The minder's hands went instinctively to his throat as his airways closed, and he took a step back.

Jack lashed out with a right sidekick, which caught him on the chest, sending him staggering back a few steps, but he refused to go down.

Spotting a fallen weapon nearby, Jack bent to reach it

coming up with it in his outstretched right hand. The minder stepped forward, anger showing in his eyes as pain wracked his features.

Jack aimed the pistol at his face and pulled the trigger.

The look of shock on the minder's face was absolute seconds before it was destroyed by a bullet passing through his brain.

Quesada went stiff as his brain shut down and he fell back to the ground.

Jack went to where he saw Charley tossed to the ground. She was beginning to wake as he knelt down at her side.

"What the fuck happened?" she asked as she recovered her senses.

"Moya is dead, and so is his monster of a minder. Now it's time we left before those Sicario out there mistake us for Moya's men."

"I saw an SUV at the side we could use. I was on my way to get it when that brute jumped me from behind. I guess he must've choked me out."

"Are you ready to move?" he asked, concern furrowing his brow.

"I'm fine," she informed him, getting to her feet.

The gunfire had stopped, and the villa had gone quiet. Jack looked in the direction of the front of the villa. A group of armed men were clambering over the rubble at the front. Moya's men, what was left of them, had surrendered by throwing their weapons away and putting their hands in the air.

Jack did a fast head count and noticed only three of them were left. Suddenly they were surrounded by more armed men coming in from the rear.

"Shit!" Jack muttered when he saw them coming

their way.

Stern faces focused intently on them as they gathered around Jack and Charley.

"Tell me you have a plan to get outta this," Charley said quietly.

"I'm working on it," Jack replied just as quietly. He made to move forward to speak to them when a bald-headed man stepped in front of him.

"Are you Jack Cross?" he asked.

Jack was taken off-guard momentarily, and his senses went instantly on high alert before he answered.

"Yes," he said guardedly.

"A friend of yours told the person we work for that you would be here and probably would need our help. It looks like we got here just in time."

"Yes, we were just about to leave. If you're looking for Moya, you'll find him upstairs. He won't be causing you any more trouble, I can assure you," Jack said.

The bald-headed man looked at the body of Quesada and then at Jack, "This your work too?"

"Consider that a favor."

Holding out a hand for him to shake, the man said, "Thank you, both of you. You have done this country a service, one that won't be forgotten quickly."

"You don't sound like Sicario," Charley observed.

"That's because we aren't. We belong to a covert unit set up to combat the cartels. I'm Major Alvarez, and this is my unit. We were contacted by your boss in England through unofficial channels as we run under the radar, much the same as your Section Zero."

"Well, it's nice to meet you, Major, and thanks again," Jack said, smiling in relief.

"You and Agent Parker had better get moving, take the chopper and head back to Charlotte. I think there might be a welcoming party waiting for you. Don't worry about this. We'll clean up here," Major Alvarez said.

They said their goodbyes, made their way out of the villa, and got into the chopper, where a pilot was waiting to take them back home.

As the chopper took off, they looked out the window at the villa as it fell away. The realization that it was over settled over them like a warm blanket. Once the villa and everything that had happened back there from the start to the conclusion moments ago had disappeared from sight, they finally began to relax.

CHAPTER FORTY-SEVEN

By the time the two agents had returned to Fairfax Airfield, it was past midnight, and they were bone tired.

It seemed like the two of them had been on the go, non-stop forever.

"Christ, what I'd give for a good night's sleep right about now," Jack said as they exited the Gulfstream to the waiting staff car on the tarmac.

"Me too. I can't remember the last time I slept," Charley agreed.

"I just hope they don't keep us too long at HQ."

They settled down in the rear seats of the Bentley staff car, but no matter how comfortable the seats were, they couldn't fully relax because they knew the coming debrief could be brutal.

The journey didn't take long, and they were soon strolling through the corridor to Bennett's office.

"Come in, you two, take a seat. Help yourself to some coffee, and there's some food as well. I thought you might be hungry. It might help you get through this next part," Bennett said as they entered his office. Two chairs had been placed before the desk with a tray of coffee and a few sandwiches on a silver tray placed on the cupboard over by the wall.

Jack poured two mugs of coffee for them and handed one to Charley. He placed a couple of the sandwiches on a side plate and brought it over to his seat for them to share.

"Now, before we start this briefing, I must caution you, Agent Parker, that what you saw here and learned about our little section here must remain a secret. This all falls under the Official Secrets Act, so you can never tell anyone about any of this, ever. Do I make myself perfectly clear?" Bennett said to start.

Jack took a bite of one of the sandwiches and chewed hungrily. Swallowing it, he turned to Charley to say, "No worries, this is just par for the course."

She glanced back at him and then turned her attention to Bennett. "Has Harper been held responsible for his actions, sir?"

"His financial records have been investigated fully by the forensic accountants of the DEA, and they found several large payments made from Moya's accounts. The fool never even attempted to hide them. He was so confident he would never be suspected."

"Does that mean I'm in the clear?" she asked.

"It does," Bennett confirmed.

"Cool," Jack said.

Charley glanced at him, "Don't ever say 'cool' again, dude. That word should never come outta ya mouth unless you're talkin' about ice cream," she admonished him.

Jack scowled at her, but he was just too tired to argue, so he let it go.

"Getting back to the business at hand, I understand you met Major Alvarez and his new unit?" Bennett said.

"Yes, sir, he was a great help," Jack confirmed.

"Sir, what happened with the antidote we gave you?" Charley asked.

"It has been distributed around all the cities we found the drones were to be used. There have been no new cases of any effect from the drug since it was distributed, and what's more, most of the cases in Miami are showing signs of total recovery. Because of your timely intervention, we managed to save thousands, maybe millions of lives," Bennett told her.

Jack saw her shoulders sag with relief.

"Sir, will there be much more? The both of us could really do with some serious shut-eye," Jack said.

Bennett nodded, "We can finish up later tomorrow. Go get some sleep, both of you. Be back here at nine tomorrow morning so we can finalize this de-brief. I'm sure Agent Parker is eager to get back to her job in the US."

"Yes sir, thank you," Charley replied unconvincingly.

Both of them rose wearily to their feet and left the office.

His own car had been driven back from Fairfax Airfield by one of the staff after his arrival there yesterday and deposited at Section Zero car park. The two of them went there straight from the office and got in.

When they arrived at his apartment, Charley turned to him, but before she could say anything, he spoke for the both of them.

"It's late. Let's just grab a few hours of kip before our

debrief in the morning. It'll save time if you stay here for the night," he said and got out of the car before she could argue.

Once inside the apartment, he said, "You take the bedroom, I'll grab a blanket and take the sofa."

Charley grabbed his arm and turned him towards her. "Don't be stupid, we can share the same bed. We're both too tired for anything else tonight, so just come to bed and relax. Besides, I'm the guest, so I should take the sofa."

"I was trying to be the gentleman here."

"Well, we can share your bed tonight, and you can play the gentleman in the morning, deal?" she countered. He was too exhausted to argue, so a nod would have to suffice.

He led the way to the bedroom, and they both went to sit on opposite sides of the bed. They quickly yet tiredly disrobed and then got under the duvet and were both asleep in seconds.

A few hours later, they both awoke more or less at the same time to find themselves entwined in each other's arms.

Jack opened his eyes to see her looking at him.

"Morning, sleepy head," she whispered as if she was afraid to break the spell.

He quickly untangled himself from her as he blurted out an apology.

"I'm, I'm sorry," he stammered.

"It's fine. I was actually quite comfortable until you just ruined it."

A smile crossed his face as he realized that it had felt natural to be waking in another woman's arms, her arms.

Discarding that thought, he got out of bed and

headed for the bathroom, muttering, "We're going to be late for the debriefing."

After each taking a much-needed shower, the two of them returned to Section Zero HQ.

The debriefing took less than an hour, it was a formality really, nothing more. When it was done, Bennett stood up from behind the desk to come around and shake Charley's hand.

"Agent Parker, you are a fine agent and a credit to the DEA. I trust your shared experience with Cross here will remain a secret. It would do neither of us any good to spread the word of our existence, and the same is said about Major Alvarez's unit in Columbia. We all have jobs to do, and we can do them better when the enemy is unaware of our existence. Do we understand each other?"

She looked him squarely in the eyes and said, "Perfectly, sir."

"That, as they say, is that then. I have no doubt that our paths will cross again sometime in the future, Agent Parker, and until then, I wish you continued success in your career in the DEA," Bennett said as he returned to his desk. As he sat down, he added, "I have arranged for a staff car to take you to Heathrow Airport, where you can catch your flight to the US. If you leave right now, I believe you will have time to catch it. Cross, you can remain here, there is something we need to discuss."

Jack and Charley exchanged awkward glances before she turned and left the office. Jack had wanted to say a proper goodbye, but it seemed that Bennett had other ideas.

He watched her leave and felt sadness wash over him at knowing he probably would never see her again despite what Bennett had said.

"Oh, don't worry, Cross. I have a feeling you'll be

seeing her again before long," Bennett said.

Jack faced the desk and stood to attention, feeling a bit silly at having displayed his feelings so openly.

"You wanted to discuss something, sir?" he asked, getting down to business.

"Yes, I wanted to formally congratulate you on the success of this mission. I can now return to the Prime Minister with my findings to inform him that this section can be a viable asset to the security of our nation."

Jack was confused, and it showed by how his brow furrowed. "Excuse me, sir, I'm not sure I understand what you're telling me," he said, wanting clarification.

"The PM wanted me to run a section that was separate from the security services, much like how Donald Bainbridge had envisioned SI6 would run, but this time it would remain under the radar. Not even the other security services would be aware of our existence. Your actions in the past few days in dealing with Moya and his threat have proven that it can work. Your involvement in the whole episode has been kept from any and all official records. Agent Parker will get full recognition for her part in this, but you were never there."

"I see, sir," Jack replied, understanding things a little better.

"Go home, Cross. Take a few days off, finish off your apartment. I'm sure there are still a few things that need sorting out, but keep your phone with you at all times," Bennett said.

"Thank you, sir," Jack replied, a little surprised that Bennett knew anything about his new apartment, then again, this was the security service, and it was their job to know everything about their personnel.

As Jack turned to leave, Bennett said one final thing.

"Cross, welcome to Section Zero."

EPILOGUE

LONDON—AUGUST 31

It was over, for now. Now he could return to looking for the Hierarchy.

As he returned to his apartment, Jack looked around to see if there was anything unusual. Nothing seemed out of place, no one was staring at him or watching without appearing to be. There were no strange cars or vehicles parked on or nearby where he now lived that couldn't simply be explained as people going about their daily lives.

The Hierarchy, if it still existed, was not watching him, not that he was aware of, at least.

As he entered his apartment, he went over the last mission in his head, reviewing it step by step. He had to admit it was good to get back to work. Major Bacon, the Armourer from SI6, had said he had been probably the best soldier he had ever worked with, which was some compliment coming from someone who had a distinguished career in the SAS. He'd also said that the reason he kept coming back, despite all the arguments he'd had with Melissa about retiring, just proved he enjoyed the work and could not envision himself doing anything else with his life. It wasn't that he was an adrenaline junkie, someone who craved danger like an addict craves their next fix, he was someone who would do the right thing no matter the cost, and it had cost him dearly. He bore that cost daily every time his thoughts turned to that fateful day when the Hierarchy sent someone to his home to kill him but succeeded in killing only his wife and daughter. That was a price he would pay every day for the rest of his life.

His phone rang, and his immediate thought was that something had happened and Bennett wanted him back at work, until he saw who was calling.

"Charley, listen, I wanted to say goodbye properly, but Bennett had other ideas. I'm sorry," he said, holding the phone to his ear.

"Don't worry, big boy. You haven't seen the last of me just yet. Besides, we still haven't had that drink remember?" she said.

"I remember," he replied, smiling. "Where are you?"

"Just at the airport. My flight leaves in an hour, so I thought I'd give you a quick call."

"I'm glad you did. It was great working with you, and I hope we can do it again sometime soon."

"That would be nice; a drink would be nicer though. You know, nice relaxing atmosphere, a single malt or three with no bullets flying around, that kind of thing."

"Over here, we call that kind of thing a date."

"A date it is then," she said without the slightest hesitation.

Jack paused for a second. He was recently widowed, but if he learned anything about his wife in all the time they spent together, all the wonderful times, it would be that she would not want him to stop living his life. They may have argued about his career choices and how it threatened their time together, but when it all boiled down to what was important, it was this. She would want him to be happy.

Agent Parker made him happy, and he felt no guilt or shame in accepting that.

He said, "I'll see what I can arrange."

"Thought you were gonna keep me hangin' there for a moment, dude," she admitted sounding genuinely relieved.

"Agent Parker, Charley, you stay safe out there," he said.

"You too," Charley replied and hung up.

Jack had no idea when they would meet again, just that they would.

He looked around his new apartment, thinking about it. It was a new beginning for him, almost like a clean slate. His past would always be with him; his memories of past experiences, past loves, but with this new beginning came new hope too. Hope that he will be happy once again. He had given himself permission to be happy, to carry on doing what he was good at, to love again.

Was Charley going to be a part of that new life?

Only time will tell.

IF YOU LIKE THIS, YOU MAY ALSO ENJOY UNIVERSITY: THE COMPLETE SERIES

by Terrence McCauley

An unforgettable series where enemies come and go, but one hero remains resilient.

In *Sympathy for the Devil*, James Hicks runs The University, a clandestine organization using its vast intelligence to strike back at terrorists all over the globe. When his brilliant protégé is turned by a terrorist group operating on U.S. soil, he must use The University's covert global network to uncover a deadly plot threatening to unleash a new era of chaos and anarchy.

Hicks and The University are caught in deadly crosshairs during *A Murder of Crows*. Every intelligence agency is on the hunt for the elusive terrorist known as The Moroccan. When Hicks and his crew capture The Moroccan, they find themselves in a strange new world where allies become enemies, and enemies become allies.

The stakes are at their highest in *A Conspiracy of Ravens* when Hicks finds his true enemy, a criminal organization known as The Vanguard. The Vanguard is a deadly organization comprised of the worst people imaginable. When Hicks uncovers a solid lead, his world explodes, and The University finds itself in open combat against an unknown enemy.

During *The Moscow Protocol*, Hicks is on the road to recovery from extensive facial reconstructive surgery when he finds one of the most wanted men in the world. The intelligence community needs him, and The Vanguard wants him dead. Forced into hiding, he must come up with a way to trap the Vanguard and end its threat to democracy once and for all.

AVAILABLE JULY 2023

ABOUT THE AUTHOR

Jack Dillon loves to write fast-paced thrillers that have plenty of action. He grew up watching James Bond films, and he read every one of the books he could get his hands on. When other authors started catching his eye—authors such as Clive Cussler, Jack Higgins and, Matthew Reilly—they inspired him to write his own adventures.

So far, Jack has written two series with strong leading characters, the Jack Cross series and the ATLAS Force series. A statistic of the pandemic, he was forced into early retirement. But it wasn't such a bad thing as it gave him the opportunity to write full time, which had been a long-held dream of his.

Living in a beautiful part of the Derbyshire peak district, Jack takes advantage of the wonderful scenery. And when he isn't gazing at it through a window, he can be found finding other ways to procrastinate. Don't worry, though, he still has plenty of ideas that will eventually find their way into a book. At least, that's what he tells himself.